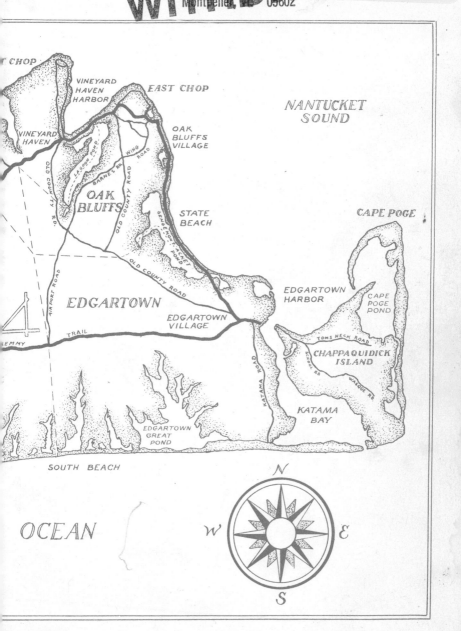

THE GAY HEAD
CONSPIRACY

BOOKS BY CARLOS BAKER

Novels

A FRIEND IN POWER
THE LAND OF RUMBELOW
THE GAY HEAD CONSPIRACY

Poetry

A YEAR AND A DAY

Criticism

SHELLEY'S MAJOR POETRY
HEMINGWAY: THE WRITER AS ARTIST

Biography

ERNEST HEMINGWAY: A LIFE STORY

CARLOS BAKER

THE GAY HEAD CONSPIRACY

a novel of suspense

Charles Scribner's Sons

New York

This book is for Catherine (ladies first)
and Brian and Stephen and Matthew
and Michael and Charlie

Chapter One

1

AS SOON as the ninth wave had crashed and receded, he stepped onto the wet sand and plunged his hands into the water. Before the next wave had gathered its strength, he jumped back, wiping his hands on his jacket. Even at this time of sunset in early October the sea water still felt warm. He considered and rejected the idea of one last swim before the night closed in, and stood for a long moment gazing around at the now familiar scene. There was Cuttyhunk low on the western horizon, with the intervening water calm and streaked with color, and the red buoy bobbing half a mile from shore. At last he turned his back on the ocean and the sky and tramped through the sea-wrack to the flat boulder where his painting equipment was spread out.

Sitting on the still-warm rock, he shuffled quickly through the sketches of the ocean and the promontory that he had made during the long afternoon. Around the corner to his left as he faced the low cliffs lay the famous headland itself, the streaked clay sides rosy now in the setting sunlight. Gay Head. No wonder they called it gay, though you couldn't be sure it hadn't been named for a man rather than a quality. Long ago, before the heavier erosion, it was said to have been gayer still. Now the colors were only chalk white, brick red, occasional streaks of yellow, and the common hues of dirt where the clay had been washed away to expose the ancient gravel.

We ruin everything, he thought, and what we don't ruin Nature does. Like forest fires started by lightning that leave a thousand acres of timber a wilderness of black skeletons. Like rock slides down the flanks of mountains, like the detritus below Niagara, like the wearing down of Gay Head itself. You accepted acts of God, and after the raw edge of destruction had worn away, the results often showed a certain barbaric beauty. But human ruination was something else again. He remembered Joe Raymond's disgust with what they had done to Fujiyama, the sacred mountain, strewn with paper and the other debris of box lunches. "We need another Spengler," said Joe, standing there beside the desk in the G-2 installation, gray eyes blazing, his upper lip beaded with sweat. "Another volume called *The Decline of the East*. Picnic trash on Fujiyama, for God's sake!" Yes, and beer cans in the Grand Canyon, truck tires in every river, oil slicks in a hundred harbors, you name it, we've done it.

But it was Nature itself, not man the destroyer, that was inexorably tearing Gay Head to pieces. Sixty feet overhead, the tufts of autumn grass loomed against the sky, the bank beneath them undercut. Soon great chunks of turf would break off and the cliff would recede another yard to landward. Huge boulders, like this one where he sat, would be loosened from beds of clay in winter gales or springtime thaws and come crashing down to litter the shore like roc's eggs.

He rummaged in his pack and brought out the other sandwich and the rest of the coffee in the thermos jug. The sunset was brighter now, an enormous spread of pastel colors, blending and reforming minute by minute, barred with high clouds like strips of gold above the island of Cuttyhunk, Indian name for something or other. But Cora hadn't been able to remember what.

Cora was the Gay Head Indian—part Indian, anyhow—who had lent him one of the small cabins she kept for summer tourists. She had insisted that he lock up his motorcycle in the weather-worn shed behind her house.

"No telling what bums might come along here," she said.

In the morning she had fried him a couple of eggs and plied him with instant coffee, a plump old widow eager for talk, her children long since grown and moved to the mainland.

"Mrs. Pease, what's the meaning of Cuttyhunk?"

"Don't mean a damn thing to me."

"I meant the name," Tom said. "It's Indian for something."

She sat round and solid in the rocker, the brindled cat in her lap, the cigarette waggling in her lips as she talked through the smoke. "Seems to me I used to know, but damn if I can recollect. You interested? I could find out."

"No, never mind. I just thought you might know offhand. I'll look it up. It ought to be in one of those Vineyard books."

She began to tell him about Moshup, the Indian giant, the one that painted Gay Head in a day, between sunrise and sunset. Nantucket was nothing but the dottle from his pipe. Another time he drew a line with one toe and when the sea rushed into the groove it made the strait between the Vineyard and No Man's Land. The dice he used for his Indian version of crapshooting were the boulders brought down in the Ice Age.

"Seven come eleven," Cora said, laughing. "Only the marks is all worn off now. They call that Moshup's Trail down along South Beach. You seen Squibnocket?"

"What's Squibnocket?"

"That's the pond down there a few miles. It was boggy and old Moshup sunk in. Made the hole where the pond lays now. They say from the air it's shaped like footprints."

The sun had already been high that mellow morning when Tom shouldered into his packstraps and crossed the field toward the dunes and the beach. Up on the height of land to his right stood the old brown lighthouse and a scattering of shacks where tourist knicknacks were on sale in summer. "Junk," said Cora, grinning. "Dolls, canes, banners, beads. Most of it made in Japan. Used to have some native-made ashtrays, red clay from the cliffs. There's one over on that table. I used to sell them before I got into the cabin business."

The path over the dunes was edged with sea-grass, bayberry, and wild rose bushes. There were also patches of poison ivy, red and purple now in the fall season. At the top of the dune the sea spread out broadly before him, flecked with whitecaps. He strolled up the beach kicking idly at the driftwood: tree roots bleached with salt and sun, planks with rusty spikes, many smaller boards—enough to stoke all the household fires from Gay Head to Chilmark and maybe Menemsha. But there was no need of fire in this October noonday. He dropped his pack and shed his jacket, sauntering on afterwards where the ebbing tide had left the sand hard-packed as any sidewalk. The cliffs grew higher as he approached the headland. Halfway along, he found the flat-topped boulder, laid out his materials, and spent the afternoon making sketches in water color, pausing once for a swim.

Now a single bloody streak low on the horizon showed where the sun had set. The lamp in the lighthouse was evidently out of commission, a casualty of an economy drive by the Federal government. Tom capped the thermos and stood up stretching. A cold wind was coming off the water. He stashed the sketches in the black folder and turned back along the beach by the route he had followed that morning. The dunes were dimly outlined against the sky and here on the shore it had turned almost too dark to see. He got the flashlight from his pack, hunched his shoulders against the rising wind, and strode quickly on.

He had gone no more than a dozen yards under the shelving cliffs when he heard the sound behind him, a heavy chunk as of something falling, striking thickly on the stones at the foot of the steep slope. A boulder, he thought. But it was not that kind of sound. Some animal, then. A cow or a deer, or one of the wild ponies that had strayed too close to the edge. He peered backwards in the gloom, holding his breath and listening. Except for the waves breaking on the beach in the freshening breeze, he could hear nothing.

He caromed the beam of his flashlight back and forth over the jetsam at the foot of the cliff. Nothing, still nothing. He walked back slowly, playing the feeble light over shapes of driftwood, hunched boulders, a dark drift of sandy seaweed.

Then he saw the cause of the sound: the figure of a man, belly down in the sand and rubble, both arms flung wide, one leg twisted beneath the body.

The man was dead. Unmistakably and finally. Tom played the light over the twisted legs, the back, the arms and shoulders. Then he recoiled so quickly that the flashlight dropped from his hand. The body on the beach was only a torso with legs and arms. The head was gone.

2

Beside the road, pines and oaks showed green-black and russet colored as the bike's headlight grazed them in passing. He was aware of old stone walls, clumps of sumac, and blank-windowed houses, closed for the season. But he ignored them, his eyes intent on the turns in the road, his helmet tight against his forehead where the headache was beginning.

At the fork he turned left downhill for Menemsha. The night air was cold on his face and once or twice he wiped his streaming eyes with the back of his hand. In spite of the lights in some of the houses, he neither slowed nor stopped. Some of them would have telephones and people willing to let a stranger use them—if the stranger explained why. But he did not feel like explaining again. Not, anyhow, until he reached the Coast Guard Station at Menemsha.

He had explained once already, for Cora's benefit, when she opened the door to his knock and found him standing there, out of breath and sweating from the uphill run across the dunes and the fields.

"Something wrong," she said, stepping back into the room. It was a statement, not a question.

"Right," said Tom. He swung the pack to the floor and wiped his forehead with the sleeve of his jacket. "Something really wrong. Have to telephone."

She had backed up further and stood with her mouth open, her old brown eyes intent behind her glasses. "I don't have no phone," she said, quickly. "You ain't hurt?"

"No. There's a dead man. On the beach. Under the cliffs."

"Maybe he ain't dead. Just took a tumble."

"He's dead all right." Tom did not want to explain the rest of it. "Where's the nearest phone?"

Cora named the filling station down the road. "If he ain't open, and likely he ain't, you could try the Coast Guard."

"Where are they?"

"Menemsha," Cora said. "Keep on past the filling station to the corners, then follow the signs for Menemsha."

The filling station was closed. Like everything else, he thought. Even Menemsha lay dark under the dim light of the street lamps: the post office and general store, the seafood place across the way, the fish shacks down by the tidal river. He turned where the sign pointed to the town dock and the beach. None of the buildings was open, but one car was parked near the bulkhead that faced the water. Its lights were on inside and the motor was running. The man in the driver's seat wore a long-billed fishing cap. He had heard the motorcycle and rolled the window down when Tom stopped and came over.

"Coast Guard?" he said. "You come past it. Back there on the knoll just off the main road. Big place. You'll see it right ahead of you. Something wrong?"

"Just looking for the Coast Guard station, thanks," said Tom.

"Feller named Monty on duty," the man in the car said. "Monty Hupp. H-U-P-P. Tell him Sam sent you."

Monty was a large strong man with a pregnant-looking belly and a pendulous lower lip. He chuckled at the mention of Sam. "You seen him down at the town dock, right? Setten in his car? Haven a beer? Readen the paper, right? His old woman won't have no beer in the house."

Tom nodded. "I don't know about the beer, but the rest

is right. Now, could I use your phone? I've got to notify the police."

Monty fixed him with a blue-eyed gaze. "Police, huh. Sam's police. You want to get the police, that's Sam."

"State Police," Tom said.

"Okay. That's Oak Bluffs sub-station. I can get them on the short wave. What did you say your name was?"

"Tom Cook."

"Now, Tom, what's the problem?"

"Problem is a dead man on the beach. Out near Gay Head."

"Drownded, huh? You found him washed up?"

"No, murdered. Head cut off and body pitched over the cliff."

"*Head* cut off?" Monty's lip drooped lower.

"Cut off—and missing. Just the—er—rest of it."

"Where was you?"

"Down under."

"What was you doing there?"

"Walking down the beach."

"When was this?"

"Today. Just at dark. Look, Mr. Hupp . . ."

"Monty."

"Look, Monty. This is for the police. Can you get the State Police at Oak Bluffs?"

"I sure as hell can," Monty said. "I sure as hell will."

Waiting beside his motorcycle at the crossroads, Tom could hear the siren for a long time before the headlights appeared and the long car pulled up beside him, the siren-scream dying like the end of a cat-call. He had just time to notice that it was an ambulance when the driver was out and approaching, a tall man with thick eyebrows and a no-nonsense look.

"You Thomas Cook? Lieutenant Milliken. Trooper Royce inside."

Royce stayed in his seat. Beside him was a large black Graflex. Tom nodded in his direction and turned back to Milliken.

"You better leave your bike here and come along with us," Milliken said.

"I'd rather not," Tom said. "Let me follow you."

Milliken looked toward Royce but made no move to consult him. "All right," he said. "Gay Head lighthouse, right?"

"No. This side of it. On the shore off that side road. The one with the Indian name."

"Moshup's Trail? Okay, we'll turn off down that way. You stay on my tail. Watch when I turn off left."

He waited until Tom was in the saddle and then started slowly. The siren began again but he cut it off at once. Tom stayed fifty yards behind the steady tail-lights. It seemed a long time before the direction signal flashed for the turn-off. A mile down Moshup's Trail Milliken stopped and waved Tom alongside.

"Somewhere along here?"

"Farther along," Tom said. "Near where the dunes stop and the cliffs begin."

"You go on ahead," Milliken said. "Take it easy."

After a mile Tom stopped and waved them down. He could see the lights of Cora's house on the rise of ground among the trees. "Here's where I came down across the field. The body's farther up the beach."

"Let's get a little closer along the road," Milliken said. "I don't want to hit the beach until daylight."

9

"Why not?" asked Tom. "You can't . . ."

"Footprints."

"They're my footprints. I was the only one on the beach."

"Let's get closer anyway."

When Tom stopped again, Milliken cut his motor and sat still. "This the place?"

"About here. The cliffs are over there."

Royce spoke for the first time. He was a thin, dark-skinned man with a long scar down the left side of his jaw. He had a Boston accent and his voice was unpleasantly high-pitched. "How high would them cliffs be?" he asked Tom.

"Fifty or sixty feet, I guess. Maybe only forty."

"Straight down?"

"No, but too steep to climb down."

Milliken had been silent. Now he spoke gruffly. "I don't like this," he said. "Suppose we all go across through that tall grass. We're taking a chance on destroying good evidence. They—somebody—threw the man over the edge. He didn't fall by himself. That means they carried or dragged the carcass through tall grass. Probably only a few hours ago. If it was daylight we could see where they went. If we go traipsing across we make a trail of our own and maybe spoil theirs. See what I mean?"

"Suppose one of us goes," Royce said. "Take that flood-light, shine her straight down all the way to the edge. That would show any mark they left. Any bloodstains. Then at the edge shine her down to the beach, check on the body, then come back by the same way." He raised his thin eyebrows and stared at Milliken, looking for a sign of agreement.

Milliken sat thinking, his fingers drumming on the rim of

the steering wheel. "Could do that," he said at last. "Could sit tight until we get enough daylight to see by. How's the tide? Any chance of the body washing out?"

"I doubt it," Tom said. "It was close in by the cliff."

"You're sure this is the place?"

"Roughly," Tom said. "Give or take a hundred yards."

"You didn't see anyone up on the cliff?"

"Nope. Too dark. And anyway the body fell behind me."

"How about taking the floodlight and shining it back and forth across the whole field?" Royce suggested. "If they left a trail, it ought to show up."

"It's an idea," said Milliken. "Maybe they had it in a car or a jeep and drove it across the field. Tracks would show. Or parked the car on the road-shoulder and the treads would show in the gravel. Harry, we could check that out, at the least. Each take one side. What time is it, anyway?"

"One-thirty," Tom said. "But I thought we came to check on the body."

"He's right," Royce said. "We can't check the field until daylight. Not the whole of it. Come back to my idea. Lemme take the floodlight and go straight across to the edge."

Milliken roused himself and swung out of the driver's seat. "Okay, Harry, where's the flood? You give it a whirl."

He stood beside Tom on the shoulder of the road while Royce, lugging the heavy floodlamp, moved awkwardly through the tall grass towards the edge of the cliff.

"Watch the edge," Tom yelled.

"I'm watching," Royce said. He set down the floodlamp and lay prone, hitched forward a few more inches, and played the beam over the cliff. "He's there," he said, presently, "but farther along."

They watched as he rose cautiously and moved along the bank—fifty yards, seventy-five. Then he knelt and lay forward, shining the light as before.. For what seemed a long time he said nothing.

"Harry."

"Yuh." His voice sounded faint because of his position and the distance.

"What do you see?"

"He's there, all right. Like the man said. Blue pants. One shoe gone, navy blue sweater."

Milliken glanced at Tom. "You hear that?"

"I heard him," said Tom. "Let's go look."

They ran through the whispering grass to where Royce lay.

"Watch this goddam bank," Royce said. "She might not hold the three of us. Now look."

He trained the beam on the body below. It lay sprawled in the circle of light. From that angle it looked more lonesome than ever. Looking down like God, Tom thought. Flotsam. No, jetsam. Thrown to bloody hell off a cliff. He shuddered, but he could not take his eyes from the Godforsaken figure until Royce shut off the light and they all stood up.

3

It seemed like a thousand years later when he sat sleepily in the straight-backed chair at State Police headquarters in

Oak Bluffs. Even the busy squawkbox in the next room had a sort of mesmerizing effect, the yammer of disembodied voices interrupted by retching bursts of static. Tom yawned for the tenth time and glanced around him.

The place smelled official, like the front room of the Coast Guard station in Menemsha where he had talked with Monty Hupp two thousand years ago. He sat idly, trying to separate out the various odors that combined to make the one he called *official*. Varnish, aging paint, linoleum, soap, some kind of oil, stale cigarette smoke, a touch of disinfectant, rank coffee simmering in a glass jug just beyond the partition. A generalized smell of masculinity, Tom thought. Honest, harsh, and a little sour.

He could not recapture that other smell at all—the sick odor of death that they had all noticed when they got down to the beach soon after sunrise. Even in the brisk morning air it pervaded the whole area. Royce had circled the body where it lay on the gray stones and brown seaweed, shooting it from all angles with the big camera. Then he had photographed and measured the cliff itself. The search for other footprints than Tom's yielded nothing.

Nothing showed, either, how the murderers had left. Up the steep and tortuous path that led to the shacks near the lighthouse? Tom and the two policemen had checked every yard of it on the way down to the beach. Nothing showed but the lingering debris of summer, a few cardboard coffee cartons, Coca-Cola and beer cans, bits of paper limp and stained after two or three months of exposure to rain and blowing dirt. If not by land, then by sea? There was no way of knowing. If he—or they—had gone by water, the high tide of the night had obliterated all the signs.

After the pictures and the measurements and a completely unproductive inch-by-inch survey of the cliff edge where the body had been thrown to the beach, they had gone over the field between the cliff and the road. But the waving grass gave no evidence of a recent passage through it, either by foot or by tires. Milliken, shrugging his burly shoulders, had brought a stretcher and a blanket from the ambulance. The body was too stiff to lie flat in the canvas sling. Both arms stuck out grotesquely. Royce spread the gray blanket over all—all but the arms and the dirty hands which looked like claws asking a question in sign language.

"God knows," said Tom aloud, just as Milliken came back into the office.

"God knows what?"

"I don't know," said Tom. "I'm not God. And thank God I don't have His responsibilities."

Milliken gazed at him sourly. "You know what I think, Tom? I think you need some sleep."

Tom grinned. "I could use some. How about you?"

Milliken slumped at the desk and drummed on the top with his fingers. "Too hopped up," he said. "Adrenalin by the quart. I'd just lay there and think. I hate unfinished business. And this is a long way from finished. You want to eat or sleep before we go on with the report?"

"No. Let's finish it."

Milliken held a cigarette in his fingers, looked at it, lighted it with a kitchen match, puffed on it twice, and ground it out. "Okay," he said. "Here's the playback." He switched on the tape recorder. For a minute there was a sound like Donald Duck in a rage. Then the voices, alternating between Milliken's crisp questions and Tom's drawling answers. Name: Thomas H. Cook. H for Hamilton. Born Ithaca, New York June 2, 1945. Educated public schools of Ithaca. Entered Cornell, Class of '66. English, math, art history. Varsity letters in soccer and baseball. Military service: drafted July 12, 1966. O.C.S. Assigned G-2, intelligence: ciphers and codes. Foreign Science and Technology Center, Charlottesville, Virginia. One year in Germany, another in Japan. Wounds, none. Decorations, none. Honorable discharge, September 9, 1968. Marital status, unmarried. Present occupation?

"Between jobs," Tom had said. "Just knocking around."

"Why the Vineyard?"

"It seemed like a good idea."

"Ever come here before?"

"Once, as a kid."

"When would that be?"

"I was about twelve. Middle fifties. My father's sister, Edith Hamilton, had a place on Water Street in Edgartown. I was there two months, until school opened again. Learned to sail, swam on South Beach, went fishing."

"Been sailing since?"

"Enough to keep my hand in."

"Where was this?"

"Finger Lakes, upstate New York. Skaneateles."

"Spell that one, Tom."

Tom spelled it. "They pronounce it Skinny-atalus, but they spell it Indian style. Like Cuttyhunk. By the way, what does Cuttyhunk mean? What's the English translation?"

"Never heard one," said Milliken. "What does Skinny—?"

"I never asked," said Tom.

Milliken clicked the switch. "That's where we stopped before. Right there at the end we were getting a little irrelevant. But let that go. Now let's get to yesterday. No, day before yesterday." He clicked the switch once more. "You came over on the *Islander*, right?"

"That's right."

"Then you made a bee-line for Gay Head. Why?"

"Not a bee-line, if you mean straight," said Tom. "I got off here at Oak Bluffs. Got some gas. Followed the shore road to Edgartown to have a look at my aunt's house."

"She still living?"

"She died long ago. The house was sold to someone, I don't know who. I rang the bell but no one answered. It looked as if somebody was living there."

"We can check," Milliken said. "So then you made a bee-line for Gay Head?"

Tom laughed. "Lieutenant, you ever watch a bee? A real bee-line is an aimless zigzag. Well, not aimless. They aim for the flowers. I zigzagged that day. Had a look at the airport. Then I got onto a road that came into Vineyard Haven. Lunch at the Mansion Coffee-house. Then I cruised around until I saw a sign that pointed Up Island. So I went Up Island."

There was a flapping noise from the tape recorder. Milliken turned it off and was absorbed for some minutes inserting new tape. "Okay, Tom," he said at last. "Let's go on with the rest of it." Under his questioning, Tom covered the night in Cora's cabin and the afternoon of painting on the beach. Boats? Yes, a few. Powerboats, mostly. "My aunt used to call them stinkboats." One steamship far out, hull down on the horizon. Any cars on Moshup's Trail? Uncertain. You couldn't hear them from the beach.

"So we come to after dark," Milliken said. "You packed up and began walking east. About what time?"

"Uncertain. Maybe ten or fifteen minutes after sunset."

"There's an afterglow. It stays light awhile."

"Not long," Tom said. "After the afterglow, say ten minutes."

"We can check the time. Any voices? Any lights?"

"No voices. The light was not burning in the lighthouse."

Milliken leaned forward and shut off the recorder. "They knew you were there," he said. "They must have seen you. The—er—body-throwing was for your benefit."

"Why?"

"Too much of a coincidence otherwise. They know you're there. They wait until just dark. They heave the body over the brink close behind you."

"But why? To scare me?"

"Could be. They don't want you on the beach. All summer there were people there every good day. But not in October."

"So they drop a headless corpse just behind me in the dark. They lie there on the clifftop and watch me come back and find it. They watch me running along the beach."

"Or was it too dark by that time?"

"I had the flashlight. They could follow that."

"They know you're going for help. They know you have got the message."

"What message?" asked Tom.

"That they are killers. Maybe even psychopathic killers."

"Why would they want that known?"

"Well, not the psychopathic part. But they know the story will hit the papers. Also the other news media. There are people they want to reach. Rivals, say."

"Rivals in what?"

Milliken's half-boyish face, topped by the ruffled brown hair, was set in tired lines. It was, thought Tom, the face of a matured boy, normally ruddy and relaxed and clean-shaven, but now graying with fatigue. You could imagine the face in better times watching a ballgame with absorption, leaning to blow the foam off a beer. But not now.

17

"Rivals in what?" Milliken repeated somberly. "That we don't know. But we'll sure as hell find out."

4

Sunlight thick as butter streamed across the bed when Tom rolled over and sat up, unsure at first of where he was. Then he remembered turning in early in the spare room at Milliken's brown bungalow. "You should sleep all right," Milliken had said. "It's a long stretch since yesterday morning."

"We covered some ground, anyway," Tom had said, yawning, his eyes already drooping. Now his watch showed that it was nearly noon. He dressed quickly and was just putting on his shoes when a telephone sounded somewhere in the house. He followed the insistent ringing down the stairs into the front hall and lifted the receiver.

Milliken sounded brisk. "Tom. Up and awake?"

"Up. Not exactly awake. Slept hard."

"No bad dreams, huh?"

"Not that I remember."

"How about some lunch? Same place as last night, Seagull Diner. Go out the front door, turn left, walk north two blocks, and you'll see it. Then I want to go up island and talk to Cora Pease."

By one o'clock they were on the road in the squad car. The good October weather was holding and the sunlight lay warm on the fields and woods. They passed the entrance to the small airport and followed the South Road for Gay Head. Near West Tisbury, Milliken gestured appreciatively at a pair of swans in a placid millpond. In the doorway of the general store in the village, a policeman was standing. Milliken waved, but did not stop.

"What about the local police?" asked Tom. "Do they know?"

"Not yet. We'll hold off awhile with them. Coast Guard knows. They're patrolling around the clock and around the island. But we're keeping it out of the papers. For a while, anyhow, keep it dark. We want to get a medical report on the headless horseman."

"Where is he now?"

"Flew him to Boston last night for post-mortem and identification. Nothing yet. All we know is he was a hippie. Age twenty or so, wouldn't you say? One dime in his pants pocket. Enough for the phone call he never made. Labels ripped out of sweater and pants. No underwear, as usual. One shoe gone. I'd sure like to locate that other shoe."

When they drove into her yard and knocked on her door, Cora Pease was watching television. She let them in, turned off the set, and came back to where they were standing. "Well," she said, "I'm glad you come, officer, and Mr. Cook, too. I got a sad tale to relate. I went out to the woodshed a while ago to get some wood. The motorbike's gone. At first I thought Mr. Cook might have come back and took it. But then I thought, 'I been here right along and he wouldn't have took it without letting me know.' "

Cora finished and sat down, an old woman close to tears. Or so it seemed until she spoke again. "You don't s'pose them bastards took it?"

Tom glanced at Milliken, who nodded quickly. "Maybe they did, Mrs. Pease. When did you notice it was gone?"

"An hour ago," Cora said. She hadn't been near the shed since the night before. Scared to go out. All morning she had watched television, switching from channel to channel, listening for a newscast about the murder. Towards noon she decided to bake a cake. She got the materials together and then went out to get some wood. The shed door was closed but the motorcycle was missing. "I never did bake that damn cake," said Cora.

Milliken made some notes on a pad at the kitchen table. All they added up to was that Tom's motorcycle could have been taken at any time between dark and dawn. He was almost certain that he had locked it when he rode it back there after the night and the morning on the beach with Milliken and Royce. They had waited out front with the ambulance. Maybe, in the stress of the moment, he had forgotten to lock it. The key, anyhow, was missing.

Cora Pease had heard nothing. Either they wheeled it out of the shed and down the road towards Chilmark or, if it was locked, two of them could have handled it easily enough. Heave the machine into the back of a pick-up truck, say, cover it with a tarp, and then take off into the wild green yonder.

"How big is the Vineyard?" asked Tom.

"They call it a hundred square miles, more or less," Milliken said.

"Plenty of room to hide something in."

"If they wanted to. And plenty of deep water all around. But my hunch is that the stealing and the hiding were a means to an end."

"Like what?"

"Like harassment. Like making things rough enough for you so you'd get aboard the *Islander* and go back where you came from."

"That's logical. They want a man to go away so they swipe his means of transportation."

"There are cabs," said Milliken, grinning. "Even squad cars. The number of squad cars was increased last summer when the hippies discovered us. Here, Tom, let me see your registration. We'll put out a bulletin on the bike. Somebody might have seen it this morning." He took the paper and went out to use the radio in his squad car.

Cora sat smoking in her rocker. "I feel terrible about that bike," she said.

"We'll find it," said Tom.

"I wouldn't count on it," said Cora. "Never had thieves before. Not that there was anything worth stealing. I hope your stuff is still in the cabin. I was too upset about the bike to think of that. You better go look. And you're welcome to stay. I wouldn't mind having a man around the place."

Tom grinned at her. "I'll stay, all right. But I'd like to find that machine."

"It looked new," said Cora.

"It was. Twelve hundred miles on it. Hardly broken in."

Milliken was standing in the doorway. "I just put out an alert, Tom. They won't try to take the bike back to Woods Hole on the ferry, anyway. All they can do is hide it or dump it overboard."

"Thanks," said Tom. "I think I'll stay out here and look around. If you don't want me for anything else."

"Not as long as I know where you are," said Milliken.

"Mrs. Pease says I can stay on in her cabin. I'll go check and see if they left my pack and my razor."

Milliken looked at him critically. "You could use a shave," he said. "While you're shaving I want to talk to Mrs. Pease about the night of the murder."

"Here," said Cora, getting up. "You better take the tea-kittle. No sense shaving in cold water."

Outside, a breeze had sprung up off the ocean. Cumulus clouds were moving majestically from west to east. Tom crossed to the cabin and opened the door. The pack was on the bed where he had left it. He laid it open, found the shaving kit, stripped off his sweater and shirt, poured hot water into the basin, and began to shave.

Milliken must be right. It could only be harassment. Pitch a corpse down a cliff behind you in the dark, then steal your motorcycle. All their skulduggery had done nothing for them so far except to get the police on their backs. Or, if not precisely on their backs, aware of them—working, as the phrase ran, on the case.

But why assume the murderers and the robbers were the same? It could be two groups, not one, the murderers trying to scare you off, the robbers tying you down by making off with your best means of getting away. The odds, though, were against the two-groups theory. If the purpose was harassment, the best method would be to keep it up in a variety of ways.

Milliken was standing in the doorway when Tom crossed from the cabin to Cora's house. "Feeling better?" he asked.

"Cleaner," Tom said. "What's on your docket for now?"

"It's early still," said Milliken. "I had an idea I'd check in with some of the town police. Here first. Then Chilmark and Menemsha and West Tisbury. You get better cooperation if you can talk to them. They know you're counting on them. They'll all get the radio alert, but that's not the same as chewing the fat a little. One of them might have seen something—"

"Like what?"

"Could be anything. Something out of the ordinary. A

22

man might not think of it unless I sort of pried it out of him. We cracked a case of boat-stealing last year just that way. They had the boat up in the woods for a repaint job. One of the damn fools came into the store for a pint of turps. Store-keeper happened to mention it to his pal, the police chief. Police chief tipped me off. We looked into it and nabbed them. How about you, Tom? You want to come along?"

"I think I'll stay around here. If they're watching from somewhere, they'll know you were here, and they'll know when you leave. If they've got any more bright ideas about harassment, they might try one tonight. I'd like to be around when they do."

Milliken's heavy eyebrows came together in a line. Under them his eyes were fixed on Tom's. "If it's Cora Pease you're worried about," he said briskly, "I can get somebody out here for the night. How about Royce?"

"If they're watching, they'd see the car. It might scare them off."

"What's wrong with that?"

"Nothing's wrong but that they might not show up. They might not show anyway. But if they do, there's al-ways a chance—"

"Of catching them?" said Milliken. "Look, Tom, this is a group. Maybe two or three, maybe more. One old woman and one unarmed man are not going to be any match for a gang in the dark."

"Maybe not," said Tom. "But we can't—I mean I don't want to leave her alone out here. Not after last night. Last night they were twenty yards from her while she was asleep. Last night they had a motorcycle to steal. They've got that. Now, tonight, what will they get?"

Milliken had come down from the steps and stood silently on the sere grass of Cora's front yard, his eyes squinting in the brilliant sunlight. At last he roused himself and looked fiercely at Tom. "Cut-throats," he said. "Literal cut-throats. Tom, where's that jacket of yours?"

"I left it in the cabin."

"Get it and come on down to the car."

"I'm going to stay here," said Tom. "I don't—"

"Put on the jacket," said Milliken. He was already moving towards the squad car. "Get a wiggle on."

When Tom reached the car wearing the jacket, Milliken was already in the driver's seat. He waved Tom in beside him. "You were in the army," he said. "Ever handle a pistol?"

"Some," said Tom.

"Here, then," said Milliken. "Stick this inside your jacket. It's not strictly according to rules, but neither is the situation. I'm deputizing you." He scribbled something in his notebook and handed it across.

"What's that?" asked Tom.

"A receipt for one Smith and Wesson, caliber thirty-eight," Milliken said. "Sign your name. I'll fill in the date."

Chapter Two

1

THAT NIGHT Tom had trouble getting to sleep. His six-foot frame overhung the old couch in Cora's kitchen, and besides he had slept fifteen hours the night before. But the chief enemy of sleep was expectation. There was no way of knowing what that other enemy—the still nameless, still faceless enemy—would try to do next.

Cora Pease did not seem to be greatly worried. By half-past nine she was snoring lustily among the old-woman odors in her bedroom off the kitchen. During supper they had watched the newscast on television, enlivened by her comments on a composite character she called Hinkly-brinkly. Later, carrying his flashlight, Tom had gone out to check the dooryard and inspect the smaller buildings behind the house. A wet fog was rolling in from the ocean and he could see nothing beyond the ghostly circle of his flashlight, like ectoplasm against the drifting fog. He snapped shut the padlocks on the shed and the first cabin, and carried his sleeping-bag into the kitchen. Cora was already nodding in her chair, with the brindled cat curled up at her feet. She came awake far enough to put the cat out, and then to pad across on slippered feet to the old cupboard in the corner, returning with a half-filled bottle of whiskey.

"I generally have a nightcap," she said, and brought two

jelly-glasses from the cabinet above the sink. She handed one to Tom, poured the whiskey, and drank her own straight. "You want some water, you know where it is," she said. "And have a good sleep. I got a feeling they won't be back." She disappeared into her room and closed the door. Before Tom had finished his drink, she had begun to snore.

There was an old copy of *Cosmopolitan* on the table by his chair. He began idly turning the pages, looking for something worth reading. After a few paragraphs he found that he could not concentrate. In spite of what Cora had said, his muscles were tense with listening. He took the flashlight and made another circuit of the grounds. The low trees were dripping with moisture, and he could hear nothing beyond the muffled beating of the waves on the shore and the faint, distant clang of the bell-buoy farther out, like a church-bell in the sea.

Back in the kitchen he left his wet shoes by the door, spread the sleeping-bag on the couch, and stretched out, with the flashlight and the gun on the floor within reach. The kitchen was warm and he slipped gradually into a doze. Once he awakened and checked the luminous dial on his watch. It was only eleven, and he settled back down, his hands behind his head, trying to think sequentially.

Milliken had supposed at once that the body had been dumped over the cliff at that time and place so that Tom would be sure of hearing it falling and would go back and find it. Otherwise, Milliken thought, it would have been too much of a coincidence. But take the other side. Suppose the murderers had *not* seen a stranger on the beach during the afternoon. Suppose they had been waiting somewhere else for darkness to close in. Suppose they planned to get rid of the body by taking it offshore in a small boat, weighting it with stones, sinking it in twenty or thirty fathoms. So they came down through the field, carrying the body from their car or truck, and threw it over the edge. Tom had surprised them by being there. They could not show a light or make a noise. They waited until he was gone. They knew now that the body had been seen, and gave up the idea of burial at sea. They left the dead man where he was and went back to where they had come from.

That was one sequence, remote but possible. It ignored a few crucial matters, such as the business of the small boat. He had seen none, heard no sounds. This sequence involved two or three people, working as a disposal unit.

But Milliken had guessed at rival gangs. One accomplished the murder and dumped the evidence over the cliff, knowing that the stranger on the beach would find the corpse, notify the police, and thus get the story into the newspapers, where they wanted it. Why? Obviously to warn off the second gang with some such message as, "Here's your boy. Take a good look at what we did to him. This could happen to you." That line of reasoning assumed that the victim—the hapless, headless hippie—had belonged to the second gang. He had been kidnapped, murdered, and crudely beheaded to scare off his associates.

All right. What had the hippie's associates been trying to do? What was there on this island that two gangs could be fighting for? Buried treasure? Tom grinned in the dark. You heard romantic stories of old trunks filled with pieces of eight, or family silver. But no Yankee sea-captain would have been foolish enough to bury a fortune in a sandy hole in the Vineyard woods. He would have converted his possessions to hard cash and put it safely away in a Boston bank to gather interest far from prying eyes and itching fingers.

Contraband liquor, then. That was more likely. Taxes on liquor were high enough now to make rum-running profitable. Assume a good-sized cache somewhere in the interior of the thinly settled Up Island region, well away from the more populous towns on the eastern shore. The owners of the cache would be Gang Number One. Gang Number Two learned where it was and moved in for hijacking. The poor hippie, caught in the middle, was captured, murdered, and dumped by the opposition. The papers would publish it, radio and television would exploit it. It would become what they wanted it to become—a warning. In the face of it, Gang Two had an easy choice: disband and disappear, or take the consequences. That theory could even explain the theft of Tom's motorcycle. Gang Two had somewhere to get to, and fast. They had lost their own means of transport in the midst of the hijacking operation. They knew where Tom's motorcycle was and took it. Long before Milliken had sent out his alert, they were in the clear. Gang One was left in sole possession of the field.

The Two Gangs theory, thought Tom, was the more comfortable one to live with. If it were true, it meant that they were gunning for each other, not for him personally. His own role was merely that of entrepreneur, the man they pitched the corpse at, the bearer of evil tidings, the witness who would be sure to notify the police, put the fact of the murder into the public domain, and scare off the opposition.

It was comfortable—within reason—perhaps. But it left at least one large question. Suppose Gang Number One did in fact have a cache of illegal liquor somewhere in the interior of the island. Why would they be foolish enough to tip off the police at all? They would have to be damned sure, even arrogantly certain, that their cache could not be found, no matter how systematic or prolonged any search might be.

Tom turned on his side. The snoring from the bedroom

had stopped, he was sleepy now, and all the fantasies began swarming in. In one of them he was seriously advising Milliken to bring a fleet of helicopters over from the mainland. Working in teams, they could survey the whole island terrain, looking for possible hiding-places, hovering over suspicious areas until ground crews could investigate. In another fantasy that grew more elaborate by the minute, the island had become a jumping-off zone for the invasion of North America by a foreign power. All the local police had been seized and killed, and their places taken by enemy agents disguised to resemble them. D-Day was set for mid-October while the country was preoccupied with the election campaign. A fleet of enemy submarines with atomic warheads was deployed in the Atlantic, ready on signal to move into Nantucket Sound, destroy Greater Boston, and establish a succession of bridgeheads along the coast. Tom was lying in a sandy trench on the Cape Cod dunes near Truro, shooting down the invaders as they came ashore.

He could not tell afterwards where the wakefulness had ended and sleep had begun. But it was from somewhere in the depths of sleep that the strange noise reached him—not loud, certainly, but loud enough to bring him up on one elbow, his mind tingling, his ears straining to catch the sound again. He glanced again at his watch. It was three forty-five. Still listening intently, he swung his feet to the floor. There was no sound but the faint creaking of the couch.

Then he heard it again—somewhere outside. Furtive, sporadic. He could not place it. He was on his feet when it stopped again. In the dark he leaned to the floor, groping for the gun and the flashlight. With his left thumb he found the flashlight button and with his right he released the safety on the gun. There was nothing, no furniture, between him and the door, and he made it in two strides. A thin current of air came between the edge of the door and the doorjamb and he stood there, listening still, for the sound that did not come. He turned the thumb-piece and locked it in place, hoping that the door would not creak as he swung it slowly open. It made no sound. He left it open and stepped out.

The fog streamed around his face. It was too dark to see, but if he used the flashlight it would make him an easy target. He stood waiting outside the door, poised and expectant, his feet wet from the sodden grass, the gun at his side with his finger on the trigger. This time it was another sound, off to the right where the shed was, a sound like crunching, hard but not metallic. He moved three steps and stopped again. Four more brought him to the wall of the shed, a blind wall, windowless, and he followed it in the dripping darkness as a blind man might do.

When he stopped once more, he knew he was close to whoever it was. A third sound, a sound like a sigh, a sound that could only come from a throat. It was near and a little below him. He raised the gun, pointed the flashlight, and flicked it on.

A great black dog stood there, staring into the light, its eyes pale as those of a blind man, a white bone on the grass between its front feet.

"Here, boy," said Tom, quietly. At the sound of his voice the dog barked once, a heavy bass from deep in his chest, and leaped off into the darkness. As soon as he spoke Tom had known that the bark would come. Nevertheless it made him jump. Now he stood there shaking, not with fear but with laughter, amid the debris of tin cans and sodden papers that the dog had left behind. So here you are, he thought, the garbage-pail commando, well-armed but empty-handed. You are sweating from every pore and your feet are wet and your quarry has fled and it is four o'clock of a foggy morning. Remember the comment of the drama professor at Cornell: "It was well known among the ancients that the daughter of climax was called anticlimax."

2

"Big black dog," said Cora in the morning. "Enough to scare the daylights out of you. Sure I know him. He's part Labberdoor and part hog. Comes from Talbot's place over near Chilmark. Runs all over the island. Name is Nix."

Tom borrowed a shovel and buried the garbage Nix had left. The fog was lifting slowly but he sweated in the humidity as he dug the hole, feeling the sun above the fog. After a while it would show like a gold coin, faintly visible through layers of cheesecloth. Like the discovery of truth, thought Tom. The hell it was. Truth was a lot more complicated. With the shovel over his shoulder he went to stand in the middle of the road they called Moshup's Trail, gazing seaward. One lone sailboat, its canvas furled, was moving north among the whitecaps far out on the gray-green water. The beat of the auxiliary was faintly audible. Whitecaps came and went before and behind it. Some poet he had read in college had compared them to the tossing white manes of coal-gray steeds. In fact they were more like huge snowflakes, landing and melting on moving gray lava. But even that image was not exact. Whatever the philosophers or the poets said, nothing was precisely like anything else.

When the sun emerged finally, he walked eastward along the edge of the macadam, half hoping to find his motorcycle abandoned in a ditch. The sun was warm on the back of his neck. Wild asters nodded beside stone walls and the sumac displayed its red-plush cones as if in pride. Overhead in the clearing sky a few gulls made raucous cries, beating their wings steadily against the rising breeze or soaring smoothly down the invisible backs of thermals.

He did not hear the car until it was almost upon him. For a moment he thought it was going to run him down and flexed his muscles for a leap to the side of the road. Then he saw that the man at the wheel was Royce, who was not in uniform and was driving an old-model Plymouth instead of an official car. Tom held his ground until the car drew abreast. Royce was alone, he was grinning, and the long scar on his jaw was as red as a new brand.

"Scared you," he said in the high-pitched voice.

"Just for a second," said Tom.

"Going some place?"

Tom's anger stirred. "Just looking for that motorbike. What are you doing out of uniform?"

"Day off," Royce said. "Thought I'd see how you was making out."

"Nothing new," said Tom, shortly. He remembered what Milliken had said on the subject of Royce. The scar had been earned in a knife fight somewhere in South Boston. "Not in line of duty," Milliken had said. "Line of duty came later. Line of—er—criminality was first." Before he was drafted, Royce had had a police record. "All small stuff," said Milliken, "but a lot of it. As a kid he got a bad start. Drunken father, sick mother, or the other way round, I forget which. Then he was drafted and made it through

32

North Africa and Sicily. He came out of it proud and willing. Might call him a retread. South Boston, farewell."

Royce sat still in his car, his thin graying hair fanned by the breeze off the water. "One lousy motorcycle on an island this size is like a needle in a stack of hay," he said.

"It wasn't lousy," said Tom. "It was brand new."

"Same difference," Royce said. He was not a companionable man. "We'll keep looking. It could turn up. You sticking around here?"

"It looks like it," said Tom.

"Uh-huh," Royce said. He put the car in gear and drove off up the rise in the direction of the lighthouse.

Watching him go, Tom wondered that he had come at all. What made a trooper on his day off drive all the way out here from the other end of the island? Milliken might have sent him. Or someone else, identity unknown. Maybe he just likes the scenery, thought Tom. Royce's car, small now in the distance, was slowly climbing the road near the tourist shacks. Tom turned away eastward once again and Royce dropped out of his mind.

The motorcycle, if they had left it around here, would be back in the meadows or hidden behind a stone wall or lying on its side in a clump of pitch-pines. Not in the roadside ditch. Probably not nearby at all. He left the road for the adjacent fields, checking, half idly and half hopefully, all the places where he himself would have hidden the machine. Half a mile, a mile, two miles along this side of the road might turn up something. There was no adequate cover on the ocean side. This was the place to look if you were going to look at all.

He had vaulted a low stone wall into another meadow when he caught the flash of blackness from one corner of his eye. He faced around quickly and dropped to one knee. Something had moved against a screen of pines at the top of the field. He stood up again slowly. The huge black dog Nix was standing in profile, still as the statue of a hornless stag, and watching Tom warily.

"Hey, Nix. Here Nix."

At the sound of Tom's voice the dog lowered his great head to something that lay between his forepaws. Whatever it was must have been heavy, for when he raised it in his mouth his shoulder-muscles bulged as he moved slowly towards the grove of pines in a stiff-legged walk. When Tom called to him again, he dropped his burden, loped off among the trees, paused once to look back over his shoulder, and then disappeared.

The carrion smell alone was enough to guide Tom to the object at the edge of the grove—a sickening odor that rose from the tangle of black and dusty hair like the fur of some curled-up animal. A woodchuck, he thought, until he turned it over with a fallen pine branch, saw what it really was, and stepped back in sudden horror and revulsion.

It was the missing head, clods of earth in the hair, eyes closed and sunken, one ear badly torn, the raw tendons of the neck exposed—the kind of thing you sometimes saw displayed on poles or spears in Asiatic or African countries. Only, thought Tom, this specimen had been buried and then dug up, undoubtedly by the dog.

But even that was not the worst, for over it all someone had painted the face of a circus clown—red nose, V-shaped red eyebrows, and a wide red upturning grin that surrounded the slack mouth in a crude and grotesque travesty of all the laughter in the world.

Tom recoiled a step and stood unmoving, gazing down while anger replaced his first emotion of horror. It was barbaric enough to decapitate a man, living or dead. But it lay far beyond the remotest frontiers of barbarism to make a circus of the crime, to insult a corpse, to add with paint or greasepaint this gross abnormal grin to the normal grin of death. Words leaped into his memory from somewhere in Shakespeare, some battlefield scene or other. "I like not that grinning honour that Sir Somebody has." A fallen knight, that one, grinning up at the stars through the open front of his casque. But this one was something else again, this grime-covered head grinning up at the sun. A lousy paint-job, thought Tom. What bastards they had been even to attempt it. Or was it meant as some kind of joke? Grinning head, laughing head. No, *gay* head, he muttered with disgust. At Gay Head. Was this what they had meant? Crime and locale of crime all in one? A graphic warning to interlopers?

He backed away from the place still further, his gorge rising. It wasn't a thing you could get used to. All your senses were powerfully repelled. But Milliken would have to be told. It was the other half of the corpse on the beach. The worse half, worse than the most macabre imagination could conjure up in a month of Sundays. But still a link in the chain of criminality. The link missing until now, this moment. Dropped from the mouth of a dog in a pleasant October field.

The dog, he thought, might come back again. Somehow the head ought to be hidden or put out of reach—lifted by the dusty hair to the crotch of a tree to wait there, grinning that clown's grin, until Milliken could be notified to come and take it away. But Tom could not bring himself to touch it. It would have to stay where it was until the word got out to Milliken.

He stood there in a turmoil of indecision. How could you

35

reach Milliken without a telephone, without a motorbike, without a car? Suddenly he thought of Royce. Maybe Royce, cruising slowly back from his trip to Gay Head on his day off, could be intercepted, could carry the message back to Oak Bluffs.

Tom ran across to the stone wall at the edge of the field and stepped to the top, balancing precariously, shading his eyes with one hand, half hoping to see Royce's car parked or moving on the road that angled down from the lighthouse.

But there was nothing to be seen. Royce was gone.

3

Astride the rented motorcycle, the fresh morning breeze from the sea in his face, he found that he was able to forget the horror of the severed head more easily than had been possible the night before, when he and Milliken had brought it back like an obscene trophy in the trunk of the squad-car in a cardboard carton that had once held canned tomatoes.

"You're a pretty fair deputy," Milliken had said. "You keep turning up evidence."

"The torso was the evidence. This was just supplementary, like a footnote."

"Or a headnote, more like," Milliken said. He took off his trooper's hat, ran his fingers through his brown hair, and put the hat back on. "And a hell of a note, too. And pretty far gone. I'll have to slap a little dry ice around it before I ship it out on the plane."

"Where's it going?"

"Where the rest of him is. The lab in Boston. Match up the two parts. See what they can do about identification. And tomorrow we'll have to line you up some transportation. You can't turn up more clues without transportation."

"I did," said Tom, grinning. "Twice."

"You could get around faster on wheels."

So now, in the bright October morning of another day, two wheels were taking him at forty miles an hour along the shore road to Edgartown. Small waves curled placidly on the empty beaches and the only sounds were theirs and his own. And the wind whistling past the ear-pieces of the rented helmet. Even when he came into the village itself, the streets and lanes were quiet, fallen leaves crisp and yellow on the sidewalks.

Halfway down Water Street was an old man with a cane, his hat slightly askew. Tom passed him and stopped, then shut off the ignition and dismounted. The old man paid no attention, still moving cautiously over the uneven brick pavement. His lean jaw bristled with two days of beard. One of his shoulders was higher than the other, and he peered at Tom over the top of his misty glasses.

"Thought we had got rid of all those things for the winter," he said.

"The bike, you mean? They get you around."

"Don't get *me* around," the man said. "Get me aroused. Dang noisy . . ."

"I wanted to ask you a question."

The old man nodded his head.

"Who owns the big white house over there?"

"Man name of Summers. Dr. Summers they call him. Big place, too. See that garden? Keeps one man going all the time."

"Not the one with the garden," Tom said. "The next one to it, the one this side."

"That one. That's Edie Hamilton's place."

"I mean who lives there now?"

"She's away. The Duchess."

"A real duchess?"

"No, they just call her that. Always traveling around."

"I was here the other day and it looked as if someone was living there."

"That's her daughter. Niece, I *should* say. Young girl. Pretty girl. Long hair. Polly. She's there some."

"Polly who?"

The old man's mouth closed tight. "Who wants to know?" he asked.

Tom laughed. "Me? Who am I? My name is Cook. Tom Cook. I'm Edith Hamilton's nephew. I used to come here in the summer when she owned the house."

The old man resumed his crab-like crawl. "Polly," he said, over his shoulder. "You go ask her."

It was a little like the end of a presidential press conference, thought Tom. Except that he had found out something. He parked the motorcycle at the curb and knocked on the door of the house across the street.

He remembered the stone flags of the front walk and the covered porch from the time of his boyhood. He had done some reading in an old khaki hammock during the daily rest periods that his aunt insisted on. But the Duchess, whoever she was, had transformed the place with expensive outdoor furniture, geraniums in ceramic urns on either side of the doorway, and a profusion of other flowers in pots and hanging baskets. There was a sound of orchestra music from inside the house, and he had knocked several times before the music stopped and the girl appeared, a dim apparition behind the screen of the door.

"Sorry I didn't hear you," she said. "How long have you been waiting?"

"Not long," Tom said. "Is that Brahms?"

"Schubert," she said. "What can I do for you?"

"I used to live here. My aunt was Edith Hamilton. My name is Tom Cook. I just talked to an old man who said your name was Polly."

The girl came out into the morning light. She was wearing a green jersey and blue jeans and white sneakers. Her dark hair was pulled back severely from her face and confined in a pony tail behind her head. "Pretty" was what the old man had called her, but it was not the right word. Beautiful wouldn't do, either. Or severe, in spite of the way she did her hair. As she stood now, less than a yard away, her trim figure erect as an arrow and her gray eyes appraising him, he thought only that she was a damned good-looking girl.

"Polly Harmon," she said. "That must have been Mr. Perkins. I see him in the supermarket. He loves supermarkets."

"He wouldn't tell me your last name. Said I should ask you."

"Well, now you have," Polly Harmon said. "And you're Tom Cook. I never met your Aunt Edith, but I've heard about her."

"I heard about your aunt from Mr. Perkins. The Duchess, he called her. She travels."

The girl laughed, a hearty laugh that showed her white and even teeth. "The Duchess is my Aunt Letitia. She loves traveling the way Mr. Perkins loves supermarkets. I'm house-sitting for her. So that settles the business of relatives. Would you like to come in?"

"Just for a minute. I don't want to disturb you."

"Do I look disturbed?"

The gray eyes were alight with laughter. Her dark hair as she turned to the door glinted cleanly in the sunlight. Five feet four, he thought. Mr. Perkins's adjective was right in one way: she had pretty ears.

The living-room was large and comfortable. Many paintings covered the walls.

"Do you paint?"

"Can't draw a straight line," she said. "I play." She waved a hand at a small piano in the corner. On the rack were some Chopin preludes. "Does it look the same as when you were here? And when was that?"

"The summer of fifty-seven, I think it was. I was twelve. There was a hammock on the porch that I used to swing in and read in. No, it's all changed. And for the better."

"The hammock's in the attic. Faded khaki, right?"

"It was faded even then," said Tom. "Well, thank you. I'm glad to meet you. You've been playing Chopin."

"Yes. This isn't much of a piano. I use the one in the next house when he's not here."

"When who's not here?"

"Dr. Summers. He has a baby grand. In excellent tune. He plays, too."

"When he's not seeing patients?"

Her laugh this time was silvery. "He's not that kind of doctor. He has a Ph.D. from Göttingen. He's a wonderful man."

"What does he do?"

"At the moment I think he's in Cambridge, working in

the Widener Library. He also travels. And writes. And goes sailing. And raises flowers."

"A man of parts."

"Yes, and what about you?"

Tom told her some of what he had told Milliken. He did not mention the headless body and the bodiless head. "I paint a little, too," he concluded. He told her about the sketches he had made of Gay Head.

"Isn't that a supreme place?" she said. "Especially about now. Wild and lonely. You must show me what you've done."

"They're only sketches. Later I might work some of them up."

"Do you know Virgil Thomson?" she said. "I've just been reading *The State of Music*. Do you know what he said about painting? Here, I was just reading it when you came." She took up an open book and ran one clean index finger down the page. "Here it is. Look. He says, 'The painter's whole morality consists in keeping his brushes clean and getting up in the morning.' "

"Well, then I'm moral," said Tom, grinning. "If that's all it takes."

They shook hands on the porch. He was glad that her handgrasp was firm. A tall man was working in the garden of the house next door. He peered at them balefully across the white picket fence.

"That's Otto," the girl said. "Hi, Otto."

Otto paused in his work long enough to lift one large hand in greeting, but the expression on his face did not change. He was deeply sunburnt, with heavy black eyebrows under the bill of his swordfisherman's cap. He continued to stare at them for a long moment before he turned his back.

"Sullen," said Tom, quietly. "With those shoulders he could be a bouncer in a bar."

"I don't know what he did before he came here," said Polly.

Whatever it was, it wasn't gardening, thought Tom. But he said nothing of this to Polly Harmon, who waved to him once as he moved down the walk and then went back into her aunt's house. It was like— What was it like? Like the sun going under a cloud, maybe. But not really. For the second time in the past few days he reflected that nothing was exactly like anything else.

4

In the afternoon he went up island to see Monty Hupp. By the time he turned the last curve and rode down the hill, the sun had gone under. Gray clouds were moving in from the west and the sea was the color of slate, slashed with purple. Monty was dozing in the wardroom with a newspaper in his lap. He greeted Tom like an old friend.

"Milliken said you was coming. Made you his deputy, huh? Found any more headless horsemen?"

"Just the head."

"Milliken said it stunk to heaven."

"Something like that. He dry-iced it and sent it out on the next plane. Now the lab men can worry about it."

"Deliver me," Monty said, pushing the air away with his huge hands. "I smelt enough stinks when I was fishing and lobstering to last me a long while. Ever smell a dead seal?"

"You must have got plenty of fresh air."

Monty cocked a blue eye, and shook his dewlapped cheeks. "Ever go lobstering in winter? Hauling them traps out of icewater? They ain't invented the glove that'll keep out *that* cold. Used to piss on my fingers to get 'em warm."

"I never thought about lobstering in winter," Tom said.

"Them winters was tough," Monty said. "Tell you another thing that's tough." He flourished the paper he had been reading. "Ever try these things? Every day in the Boston paper. They call 'em Jumbles. You got to unjumble four words and then make another word with some of the letters. That's the answer word. Says here what the clue is: how twelve dozen fat people look."

He handed the paper to Tom and leaned over to point a huge forefinger at the scrambled words: SUOMY, RORIP, PAHSIM, and TORGOT. "Today ain't my day," he said. "I can't seem to get a one of them."

"Suomy must be mousy," said Tom quickly. "Those others look like prior, mishap, and grotto. Now you take the letters in the circles and put them together, right? G-R-O-S-S. That's how twelve dozen fat people look: gross."

"Jehosaphat!" Monty cried, admiringly. "Milliken said you was a code man."

"Codes and ciphers," Tom said. "You get used to solutions. Any more you can't get?"

"I got yestiddy's," Monty said. "Took me jest a mite longer than you took."

"In code and cipher work they sharpen you up with four or five puzzles before breakfast."

"Jumbles for breakfast," Monty said. "Didn't they use to have—howdy, Marge."

A large woman had entered the wardroom. She was

wearing a print dress with a design of maple leaves in red and brown. Five eight, Tom guessed. A hundred and eighty pounds. Long legs, muscular calves. Red hair and glasses. Ten years younger than Monty.

"Marge, come shake hands with Tom Cook. This here's my wife Marge."

Tom rose as she crossed the room. Her hand was large and hard as a man's. Her dentures gleamed. "Pleased to make your acquaintance, Mr. Cook," she said, politely.

"Thank you," said Tom. "We were doing Jumbles."

Marge Hupp patted her husband's head. "Monty can't hardly wait for the paper when he's home on liberty," she said. "Every morning he wants his Jumbles. When you getting off, Monty? I thought you'd be all spruced up and ready. We got to get some groceries."

"Bolduc called up," Monty said. "His wife ain't feeling well, or so he says. Wants me to cover for him until after supper."

"Then I'll do the marketing and wait supper for you," Marge said. "You got a couple ten-spots on you?"

Leaning forward in his chair, Monty extracted a worn billfold, opened it, wet his thumb, and counted out three tens. "Get a steak if you see a good one," he said.

When Marge had gone, Monty leaned forward confidentially. "Ain't she something?" he asked. "Smart, too. Used to teach school. Now you take most of them, they'd squawk when they had to change plans. You take my first wife, you had to start building up to something twenty-four hours ahead, and even then you was never sure what she'd do. This redhead's different. 'I'll go along to the A and P and wait supper 'til you get home,' she says. Some redhead."

Tom said that she was a very fine woman.

Monty seized his pendulous lower lip between a thumb

44

and forefinger. For a minute or two he seemed lost in thought, but his blue eyes were like steel gimlets when he turned them on Tom again. "Good in bed, too," he said, matter-of-factly. "Built for it. Jest as soon have it afternoons as nights. Marge don't care for it in the mornings and I don't."

"I see what you mean," Tom said, wishing that Monty would change the subject. He had seized the big lower lip again and his eyes were veiled as before.

"Come to think of it, how'd you get over here?" he asked suddenly.

"Rented a motorbike from Crowley at the Bluffs."

"Yours still missing, huh? Them bastards steal the gold out of your teeth while you was asleep. Hippies. We sure had a raft of them last summer."

He told Tom how a crew of them had tried to pitch tents on government property, refusing to move even when he went out and argued with them politely. They said they were citizens of the U.S.A. and that government property was their property. "They had a point," said Monty. Finally Captain Snow, the Coast Guard Station C.O., had to go out and threaten them with a pistol before they pulled up stakes and left. Some of them went over to the beach near Gay Head and built themselves a few shacks out of logs and planks and assorted driftwood. "Like little doghouses," Monty said, "and they tell me they smelt like fox dens. A few was more elaborate. I seen one where a feller was shacked up with a girl. Along about first light they come out of there hand in hand, nekkid as jaybirds, and went down to take a wash."

"Where were you?"

"Oh, me? I was offshore with the highpower bernock-lers," Monty said, grinning. "Doing my duty, you might say. She wa'nt much to look at, anyhow. Doing my duty on the old dawn patrol."

"Are you still patrolling?"

"Sure as shooten. After you found that body, Milliken wanted a ring patrol around the whole island, and around the clock. They sent over a couple of fast service launches from Woods Hole, but of course you can't cover an island this size with a dozen of them. All anybody has to do is sneak in to shore after the patrol has gone on past. Or come at night, if they know the coast or if there's moonlight. But our guys got orders to stop any craft that looks suspicious, and if they don't stop, fire acrost their bows. And to board and search. Sometime they might find your motorbike that way."

"I wish they could. In fact I wish they had. Have the sea patrols found out anything?"

"I been on some myself. Not a thing."

"How about the local police? Your friend Sam, for example. What has he been told?"

"He's keeping an eye out for your bike. He ain't been told about the hippie. None of them have been. Milliken still wants to keep that quiet. My guess is things is going to stay quiet. Them murderers has either gone off the island or else they're laying low."

"Milliken thinks it must be rival gangs," Tom said. "The murderers planted that corpse behind me, knowing I'd hear it, find it, and report it. Then when the news came out in the papers, the other gang would get the message and be scared off. If that's so, the murderers must be tired of waiting."

Monty Hupp wagged his head until his jowls quivered. "Them fellers ain't waiting for nothing. Going on about their business, whatever it is—rum-running, dope-peddling, or what-all. Them's pros, and the thing about a pro is he goes on until he's stopped. And he ain't never stopped. Like them Rooshans up on the Grand Banks draggen up our fishnets. Stop 'em one place they go drag in another." Under their triangular lids Monty's sea-blue eyes were flashing with cold anger.

He's got the vision of evil, thought Tom. Or *a* vision of evil: its irrepressibility, its endurance, its constancy, its spread. Just as he has his vision of what constitutes the good life, with that big wife of his, and his snug house in the lee of some hill, and the daily Jumbles and the television programs and the sirloin steaks and the rest of it. The first vision is a threat to the second—maybe not for him personally, but still it's a threat. Thinking of it brings him to anger, and the eyes of this kindly man flash with it.

But if it was a vision, Monty came hastily out of it when the sound of a slamming car door outside made him lean forward to glance through the window.

"Here's Bolduc acoming," he said. "His wife must be better now. Or as good as she'll ever be." His homely face contorted into a smile. "Why don't you come have supper with me and Marge? She might have found us a steak. I could use one about now. How about it?"

In the minute that elapsed before the thick-set figure of Bolduc appeared in the doorway, Tom ran through the roster of the islanders he knew: Milliken and Royce still waiting for word from the lab in Boston, Cora Pease watching Hinkly-brinkly report the evening news, old Mr. Perkins nodding in his chair in Edgartown. And the girl. What would she be doing now? Sitting at the piano in her aunt's house playing Chopin. Whatever was going to happen would not happen tonight. There was a feeling of hiatus, a

sector of time devoid of revelation. He nodded back at
Monty Hupp and said that he would be glad to come to
supper.

5

At Monty's place, a white frame house with peeling paint
and front windows giving on a seascape, it was not a steak
but stuffed pork chops, accompanied and followed by beer.
Around nine o'clock the telephone rang in the front hall.
Monty's wife Marge came back to say that the caller was
Bolduc at the Station. Milliken was in his office at Oak
Bluffs and wanted to speak with Tom Cook.

"I told him you was here," Marge said. "You can phone
Milliken from here. Right there in the front hall."

"I'll go over there, instead," said Tom. For the past half
hour, as the conversation waxed and waned, Marge had
been half rubbing, half caressing Monty's broad back. It was
time to leave them alone. He said his thanks and goodbyes
and straddled the rented motorcycle.

The night was dark and chill but there were many stars.
Except for one old panel truck chugging up island, he met
nothing on the road. Milliken was reading at his desk, an
empty coffee-cup at his elbow, and the office filled with the
smell of cigar-smoke.

"Thought I'd let you know, Mr. Deputy."

"You found the motorcycle?"

"Not yet. But the boys in Boston think they have a posi-
tive I.D. on your corpse."

"That was fast."

"What clinched it was the head. The teeth, I mean. They got a tentative from Missing Persons. But it wasn't until the head got there that they were able to round up the kid's family dentist. I guess they lent him a clothespin for his nose and he went to work. He recognized his own bridge-work."

"Bridgework on a kid?"

"Bridgework on this kid. Several years back he knocked out most of his front teeth on a curbstone. Thrown out of his convertible."

"So he wasn't a hippie."

"He was a hippie all right. Seems he joined the flower children sometime after the accident. Graduated from Harvard last June. Barely. Since then he hasn't darkened the family door."

"Who was he?"

"Kid named Freddy Starr. Of the Concord Starrs. After he disappeared they waited all summer to hear from him. No word at all. Around Labor Day they reported him missing."

"A month ago."

"Roughly a month, yes. Sometime in his sophomore year this kid began playing around with drugs and got hooked. We used to call it snowbound."

Snowbound. What a descent from the days when the word conjured up only the image of John Greenleaf Whittier, the gentle Quaker poet with the clean white beard, and those mornings when you woke up to find the whole village buried under two feet of glistening snow.

Snowbound, he thought. We have come a long way down since those days. Or have we? This sick feeling of descent may be nothing more than a historical fallacy, the

49

grand sentimental illusion that things used to be better than they are now. Who knows how many retired sea-captains in the China trade were hooked on opium or secret drinkers of laudanum? For that matter, who can possibly guess how many neurotics and psychotics lay in hiding behind the beautiful bland masks of houses in those snowbound New England villages?

"There are still a lot of unknowns," Milliken was saying. "Why did Freddy Starr come to the Vineyard? And how long had he been here? And where did he live? And how did he get mixed up in whatever it was that led to his murder?"

His gray-blue eyes stared fixedly at Tom's, and there was a heavy crease of thought in his broad forehead.

"Of course you have plenty of ways of checking," said Tom quietly.

Milliken sighed, and then pursed his lips in a tuneless whistle. "Plenty of ways," he said. "And every last one of them takes a long time. You couldn't begin to guess how long. Or maybe you could. Take last summer. We had hundreds of Freddy Starrs, and Frederikas, too, all over the place last summer. Sleeping on the beaches, in the pine groves, even in the bandstands in the parks. Sitting on rocks and stone walls playing their guitars and flutes, or else hiking or thumbing along the roads with their knapsacks and those high laced rawhide work shoes that even the girls wore."

"Good kids," said Tom.

"Sure they were good enough kids, most of them. A few not, but most of them were OK. Sitting around in circles like a bunch of Indians with a peace pipe, only what they were smoking was pot. But the numbers! Like a plague of locusts over from the mainland. And now we have to check out this one because he stayed too long. Now we have to find out when, where, and why."

"How about who?" Tom suggested.

"Who done it, you mean?"

"Yes," said Tom, "and my guess, for what it's worth, is that it had to be a gang. Probably drunk when they did it. I can't see just one murderer doing that sort of hack job."

Milliken's large and boyish face tightened into a grin. "With a sharp ax," he said, "one really determined character can accomplish quite a lot. Take Lizzie Borden for one. And one single serious operator with a jeep could have done that dumping job over the cliff. You say drunks. I say psychopaths. It could even be someone that never harmed a fly in his life and then, suddenly, for some reason, he goes on a rampage."

Tom lowered his voice. "What about Royce? Where is he now?"

"Nobody's around here," said Milliken, "if that's what you mean. What's on your mind?"

"Royce. He showed up in his old car off duty out at Gay Head the day I found the—"

"The head, yes. And you think he was out scouting for it?"

"Could be. But not necessarily. If the murderer was still skulking around those parts, it could have been that—"

Milliken took up the end of Tom's sentence once again. "That Royce was out to meet him?"

"Just a speculation," Tom said.

Milliken, his brow creased, sat slumped in his chair, his hands behind his head, his eyes fixed on a cobweb in one corner of the ceiling. "All right," he said. "Let's speculate." The war, he said, had made a difference to many of the tough kids. Not all, but some, and Royce was among them.

The big thing was that they were not used to decency. Therefore indecency could not surprise them: they knew something about the forms that human bastardry could take, had lived near enough to murder and mayhem, stabbings and wife-beatings, brawls and stompings in streets and bars, petty thievery, looting and rape, and the so-called crimes of passion, so that they knew by previous initiation the whole range of anarchy and violence, accepted it as a fact of life.

So in basic training one major problem was already overcome for draftees in this group, Royce's group. From childhood they had known all about the doctrine of getting the enemy before he got you. They still had to be taught obedience, loyalty, honor, team-work, and the rest. Slack muscles and hollow chests had to be tautened and filled out. Some of them, naturally, were hopeless and remained so: liars and whiners and goldbrickers who would do anything for a discharge, dishonorable or not. But Royce was not in that group. He was one of those whom the service improved and rehabilitated. After the war he finished high school and two years of business college, married in the Church and began to raise a family, got into police work as a rookie with the Boston force, and served ten years, mostly in traffic control, before he applied for the State Police. His record was good enough. "I doubt if he's mixed up in this murder," Milliken said, "or the Gay Head conspiracy, if it is a conspiracy. He's been out here four years, his kids are in school, his wife is fat and sassy. I don't think he'd throw all that away for whatever this thing is. But it could be. It's happened before."

"I didn't mean—," Tom began.

"You didn't mean it was Royce necessarily, right?" The telephone on Milliken's desk rang stridently. He ignored it for the time it took to finish what he was saying. "You

52

didn't meant it was Royce," he repeated, raising his voice against the sound of the bell. "All you meant was it *could* be Royce, and I've admitted that. Excuse me." He lifted the phone and said his name. In the quiet of the office Tom could hear the tinny torrent of talk from the other end, and Milliken's monosyllables, like marks of punctuation.

"Well, good," said Milliken at last. "Tell Harry I said good work. And thanks. Right. So long." He replaced the phone in the cradle and swung around to face Tom.

"Speak of the devil," he said. "That was the chief at Woods Hole. They've got your motorbike. They think it was taken over in a small boat. We've been watching all the ferry-boats and it never turned up there."

"Who's the devil?"

"Oh, I meant Royce. He's over there in Woods Hole. He was the one that spotted your bike."

"Where was it?"

"Parked in an alley behind one of the lobster places. The key was in it but it was out of gas."

"Damaged?"

"Apparently not," Milliken said. "Royce hid under a flight of stairs and waited over an hour for the thief to come back. No luck. So he took a chance and left his hiding place to telephone the local police. Then he went back and hid again. In about five minutes someone came into the alley. It was too dark to see who it was, and Royce didn't have his gun or his flashlight with him. He waited until the character was close to the bike and then went out after him. He wasn't fast enough. The other one had a five-gallon can of gas. He threw it at Royce and ran. There's a space at the end of the alley where the two buildings almost meet. He wormed through there and got clear."

"The thin man," Tom said.

"He couldn't have been fat," said Milliken. "That was when the police came along. They've got the gas-can, presumably with finger-prints, and they've dusted the bike for more prints. But no thin man, at least not yet."

"Have they checked the gas-stations for sales?"

"Only one was open at that hour. He hadn't sold any gas. Sometimes with an old pump you can lift up the outside hood and steal gas late at night. It's been done. Anyhow we'll know a little more tomorrow. They're sending the bike over on the ten o'clock boat. Can you be there when it comes?"

"You bet."

Chapter Three

1

THE MORNING sea was choppy and cold, like something carved from liquid granite. Gulls wheeled in the wind with their lonely-sounding cries. A dirty fishing-boat chugged past, the owner in yellow oilskins. Around the ferry slip a few men worked quietly among the boxes and bundles. One of them, wearing a red-checked lumberjacket, was chalking something on a pinewood crate. Still others, all of them with their hands in their pockets, stood gazing seaward, their shoulders hunched in the face of the cold breeze that came off the leaden water. Tom stood with these, unspeaking, unspoken to, a little apart, incurious, ungregarious, content to be there without joining those who in their turn gave no sign of wanting to be joined.

The *Islander* had just appeared, white against granite gray, aggressively shouldering the waters aside, when Tom felt a hand on his sleeve and heard his name.

It was the girl, Polly Harmon, in a navy peajacket over blue jeans and sneakers. She had tied up her black hair behind her head with a bright red ribbon that nearly matched the glow in her cheeks.

"I thought it was you, Tom Cook." She was looking up at him cheerfully. He noticed for the second time the delicate molding of her nose and cheeks and ears, and for the first time the determined set of her chin and the full firmness of her mouth which might, like the way she wore her hair, have seemed too severe without the softer aspect of the rest of her face. "What brings you here?"

He smiled down at her. "I'm meeting a motorbike."

"With somebody on it?"

"No. I mean it's mine. It's being returned. It was stolen last week."

"Stolen? Where?"

"Out near Gay Head."

"But you had it that day you came to the house."

"That one was rented. This one is mine."

"Did you find it—where?"

"Parked in a dark alley in Woods Hole. The police picked it up last night."

"I wish it had been at Gay Head. That's a lovely place. I'd have helped you find it. But instead it's coming back on this boat."

"I hope it is. It's supposed to be. Come meet it with me."

"I'd love to, but I have another meeting. Dr. Summers."

"Your next-door neighbor. I remember. A wonderful man, raises flowers, has a doctorate from some German university."

"That's the man. His car's in the shop. Seems to me it's always in the shop. This time it's in Falmouth, waiting for a spare part."

"And he's coming back from working at the Widener and wants a lift home," said Tom, quickly.

The girl nodded and smiled.

The man in the red shirt was dropping the chain at the entrance to the ferry slip. Three cars drove off, followed by a dozen people, most of them looking cold and resolute. Polly waved at the tallest of the group, a slender man with the stooped shoulders of a scholar and a full head of iron-gray hair. He detached himself from the others and hurried in her direction.

"How are you, Polly?" he said, coming up. "How nice of you to meet me." He seized one of her hands and bent to kiss it. "I have got you out on a cold morning. Your hand is cold."

"So is your nose," said Polly. "This is Tom Cook. Dr. Summers."

"I am honored," Summers said. He shook hands British fashion, a single pumping downward grasp. His accent was also English, but in the few sentences he said afterwards there were occasional Germanic intonations—the aftermath, Tom thought, of his time of study at (where was it?) —Göttingen. A wonderful man, Polly had said. He was certainly urbane, though with a touch of that stuffiness and pomposity that often appeared in German academic types. But Summers was an English name, like the accent. He carried a brown attaché case and over one arm a voluminous tweed garment that might have been a cape. Already he was sweeping grandly in the direction of Polly's car, a two-year-old Chevrolet that he evidently knew well, for he wrenched open the door, dropped case and coat on the front seat, and turned, arms akimbo, to see where Polly was.

She had hung back for a final word with Tom. "Do you ever go back to Gay Head?" she asked. "It's my favorite place on the whole island."

"Tomorrow," said Tom. "There's an old lady named Cora Pease out there that I want to pay a call on. This gray weather is supposed to blow over and the prediction is for fair and warm. Can you ride pillion? I'll come and get you tomorrow morning."

"Come around ten," Polly said. "We can go in my car.

Wouldn't that be better? I'll pack a lunch." Her merry eyes were searching his. "Don't look so disappointed. I'll ride pillion if you'd rather. But if it's warm I was thinking of wearing a dress. You've never seen me in a dress, but I do own a few."

"Let's see how the weather is when I come," Tom said. "You look fine right now."

Dr. Summers had entered the car and sat staring straight ahead, his long fingers drumming on the attaché case. As soon as Polly slid behind the wheel he turned towards her, talking volubly and (it seemed to Tom) possessively. Even when Polly waved and smiled in Tom's direction, the doctor kept on talking, and with an intensity that could have only one purpose, to divert the girl's attention away from Tom and towards himself.

He had nearly forgotten the motorcycle until Harry Royce came wheeling it slowly across the rusty lip of the gangplank. "Here she is, Tom," he shouted in his high-pitched voice. "Don't she look like yours?"

"It's mine, all right," Tom said, his hand on the saddle. "And nothing wrong with it. I was afraid they might repaint it, or change the license."

"Neither one," Royce said. "Maybe they figured on getting it well inland before it was recognized."

"And you recognized it."

"Not me," said Royce. "One of the police over there spotted it just after dark. He was doing a routine check on an empty house and there it was standing behind the hedge. He pulled up a little ways down the street and reported it on his radio. When he went back on foot, the machine was gone. Evidently the thief saw him and moved it. I was at the station chewing the fat when the word came in and I went along over. There's a lot of little streets and alleys around that section. In ten minutes I found it."

"Then the thief came back with the gasoline."

"I almost had him, but it was too dark, and that damn gasoline-can hit me right in the gut when he heaved it. So he got away through a narrow space at the bottom of the alley. We don't even have a description except that he must have been skinny as a kitchen match to get through that place."

"But you recovered the machine."

"Here she is," Royce said, proudly. "All gassed up and ready to roll."

"Get aboard," Tom said. "I'll ride you home. Maybe Milliken has a medal."

Royce grinned like a sheep. "I don't want no medal," he said. "I got a medal."

"Which one?"

"Purple Heart," said Royce. "And I got a purple gut where that gas-can hit me. No, I better walk. Got a few errands to run. Tell Milliken I'll check in at noon."

When Royce had limped out of sight around the nearest corner, Tom mounted the motorcycle and depressed the starting pedal. The engine roared obediently and he ran it a full minute before turning it off again. Back in business, he thought, and good to be back. Royce the doubtful suspect had turned out to be Royce the hero. And there was the date with Polly Harmon tomorrow, and the chance to check on the welfare of Cora Pease, whose lined old face would light up when she saw the motorcycle. But perhaps, after all, it would be better to go out there in Polly's car. His sleeping bag and the painting equipment were still in Cora's cabin, and there would be no room for Polly if he brought it all back to Oak Bluffs to stash away in Milliken's bungalow until he found another place to stay at this end of the island.

"You're welcome to the room," Milliken had said. "I'm hardly ever in the house. Plenty of sheets and towels in the hall closet."

Tom had nodded his thanks. He would stay on there until—what? Until the murderer or murderers of Freddy Starr were found? That might take all winter. If Polly stayed on the Vineyard it could be a very good winter. He tried to remember her face exactly as it had looked half an hour ago: the gray eyes and black hair, the quick smile. If the pompous Dr. Summers were really jealous, or if he was merely assuming the role of the guardian neighbor against the intrusion of unwelcome strangers, so be it. Whatever his state of mind might be, Tom thought gleefully, the good doctor would not be going with Polly Harmon to Gay Head tomorrow.

2

She was wearing a dress when she answered the door and he caught his breath when he saw her in it, lithe and high-breasted, with excellent legs and the same proud athletic walk he had noticed before. She handed him a large wicker lunch-basket, picked up a green sweater and a bunch of keys from the chair by the door, and followed him onto the sunny porch.

"How do we go, pillion or Chevvy?" he asked.

"Would you mind taking the car? It's a long way and I've never been on a motorcycle. I might fall off."

"You'd have to hug me around the middle," Tom said.

"That would be nice but let's postpone it," she said without coyness. "Do you mind?"

Tom grinned. "Only for as long as it's postponed."

"Then you'll want to lock up your bike. There's no garage, but you could put it in the back hall."

She led the way around the corner of the house and held open the wide screen door. The motorcycle looked enormous in the narrow back entry. She double-locked the door and led the way through the kitchen. "Do you remember the kitchen?"

"I remember the room but it's all modernized."

"Letitia said the old one was medieval. Not charmingly medieval, just medieval. No cook would work in it."

"There was a medieval table here by the window," Tom said. "I remember eating breakfast and looking out."

"It's still a handsome view," she said, lifting the curtains. "The garden next door and then the patch of water through the trees."

Tom bent to look. "And the great Dr. Summers, too."

"Oh, is he there?" Her head came close to Tom's and he caught her pleasant fragrance. "He appears around ten, when he appears at all, to smoke a morning cigar and peer at the flowers. And to boss Otto."

"No bossing today. No Otto."

"Otto's gone to Falmouth to pick up the car."

"Otto drives for him?"

"Yes, and digs the garden and cuts the hedges and carries home the groceries."

"He looks more like a body-guard."

"He could be, I guess, if Dr. Summers needed guarding. There, see, he's going back to his study. Shall we leave? Are you ready?"

"All ready," said Tom. He did not try to keep the note of elation from his voice. Something had already happened between them, tangible as an electric current. Or was it only on his side? But the feeling grew stronger on the drive to West Tisbury. While she handled the car well and drove fast, she talked as easily as an old friend. At the edge of the village, the swans still coursed placidly on the surface of the millpond.

"Like the swanboats in Boston," she said, smiling. "One of the overpowering joys of my childhood."

"There's a place like that in Germany. In a park."

"You've been to Germany? Where?"

"Grafenwöhr. But the park wasn't there."

"Graf—what is it?"

"Grafenwöhr. It's a training-ground over near the Czech border—big rolling plain. It's where Rommel licked his Afrika Korps into shape for the desert war."

"Then we licked them, didn't we?"

"After a while," Tom said, "and after a fashion and after gallons of blood."

"It isn't a desert, though? I mean in Germany."

"No. The whole region is very diversified, which is why they chose it several generations ago. Some of it's very handsome."

"Like the Rhineland?"

"Well, no castles on crags, though there are some crags around it. Small rivers and then fat hills with pine forests. It reminded me of the Berkshires or the Adirondacks. Good country for maneuvers. For armor. We used it for that."

"Who did?"

"The Seventh Army. You need a big place for an army."

"For how many?"

"Two hundred thousand. Maybe more sometimes."

"Wow," she said. "Why so many?"

"In case of attack from the East."

"What did *you* do?"

"Do you want to be bored?"

"No, but I asked."

"Well, we had to know the disposition of our anti-aircraft rockets and the medium-range nuclear weapons. We monitored radio transmissions and at the battalion level taught the troops how to encode tactical messages and how to confirm information that came in by radio or field telephone."

"You're trying to make it sound dull."

"It was, a little. Some of it. The codes were low-level. The fun we had was with high-level ciphers. And the Colonel's honest-to-God spy stories."

"*That's* not dull," said Polly. "You'll have to tell me more. Grafenwöhr sounds like spy country. Mysterious and faintly sinister. Now we're coming to Chilmark. Doesn't that sound mysterious, too? And faintly sinister? During the cold war I used to dream of foreign spies living quietly in Chilmark, disguised as natives."

"Chilmark looks more like Babenhausen," said Tom.

"What's Babenhausen?"

"The farm village I lived in when we weren't at Grafenwöhr. It was even neater than Chilmark." He told her about the patchwork of carefully tended rectangular fields, and the strictly disciplined forests, and the bundled faggots of twigs and small boughs, the new potatoes and the fresh brown eggs and the perpetual fragrance of cowdung.

"Babenhausen sounds like the Brothers Grimm," she said.

"So would Gay Head if you put it into German. How far is it now?"

"Gay Head? Six or seven miles. A little more if we go by Moshup's Trail."

"Could we stay on the South Road?" asked Tom. "That will bring us to Cora Pease's house, and I've got some pieces of equipment that Cora Pease has been keeping for me ever since the—"

"Ever since the what?"

"Ever since I came to the Vineyard," said Tom. He did not want to tell her about Freddy Starr. That could wait for another day. The morning sea shone bronze and blue in the distance, and the breeze through the car window tossed Polly's dark hair. He described Cora Pease and the night in the dripping fog and his first adventure with the black dog Nix. "Captain Cook, the garbage-pail commando," he said, and she was still chuckling when they turned off the road and climbed the dusty rise to Cora's house.

When Tom introduced them, Cora held Polly's strong and slender hand for a long minute. "It didn't take you long," she told Tom. "Last time you was alone on a motorbike. Now you got a pretty girl and a car."

"The car belongs to the pretty girl," said Tom.

"What about your bike? Did they ever find your bike?"

He told her about Harry Royce's recovery of the motorcycle.

"Well, good for him," Cora said, pursing her lips. "How about the murder?"

He glanced at Polly, whose gray eyes had widened at the word. "Still unsolved," he said, quickly. "They're working on it. I thought I'd take my luggage, Mrs. Pease."

"Cora's my name."

"Well, Cora. The sleeping-bag and the rest."

"Sure thing," Cora said, getting up. "It's all in here. I

brought it inside to keep it safe. There's noises outside some nights."

"How often?"

"Not every night but often enough to bother. I don't care for it, but as far as I know they haven't broken into the cabins. And then there was that car."

She told them about a car that had stopped two successive nights on Moshup's Trail. Late, around midnight, both times. It was too far away to be sure it was the same car, but each time they had driven off the road and parked on the grass and stayed there for an hour or more. It could have been neckers, Cora said, using the old-fashioned word. But then there was that thing about the lights. Every so often the headlights would blink, on and off, on and off.

"Towards you?"

No, Cora said. Out to sea to the west. She could make out the light shining on the grass.

"Any answering lights from the Sound?"

Cora shook her head. She had seen none, but that didn't prove a thing. Her old eyes were none too sharp, and anyhow she couldn't see the whole sweep of water from her front door. Some of the cabins were in the way.

"I'll tell Milliken," Tom said. "If they're bothering you, he'll want to know about it. Maybe I'd better come back here for a few nights and see what happens."

"Bring your girl," Cora said. "I'll put her up. She's a sight for sore eyes."

Back on the South Road driving towards the brown lighthouse, Tom looked across the front seat at Polly, who had said nothing for several minutes and seemed to be intent on negotiating the curves in the winding road. "A sight for any eyes," he said, softly.

She did not look in his direction or try to keep the edge from her voice. "Blarney," she said. "Pure blarney and balderdash to keep my mind off the murder. What murder did she mean?"

"Wait until we stop and I'll tell you."

"You mean it's too horrible and I might faint and drive us into the ditch?"

"Maybe not. But I'd rather tell it with fresh air and good scenery."

They parked near the lighthouse and walked to a place near the edge where the great streaked cliff fell away to the shore far below. "We might as well sit down," he said. "It's a long story."

Somewhere in the midst of it she took his hand. Afterwards she sat silently, gazing out over the expanse of glittering water for what seemed a long time.

"What a horror for you," she said, at last.

"The head was the horror. With that clown face. I still see it in my dreams."

"Gay head. Ugh! A real sick joke. In a thousand years I would never have thought of that."

"Someone did. It was the dirtiest trick of all."

"What's dirtier than decapitation?"

"It's bloody enough. But let's stop. I hadn't meant to tell you."

She had taken away her hand to smooth her windruffled hair. "You mean not ever?"

"Not yet, anyway."

"Does it really haunt you?"

"Not enough to spoil my appetite. Where should we eat? Up here or down on the shore?"

"Can you find that big rock where you were painting that first day?"

"It's probably just where I left it."

She stood up and brushed the dried grass from the back of her skirt. "Let's go there," she said. "And please bring your paintings."

3

The rock was warm from the sun. Small waves broke placidly on the pebbled beach. Offshore a pair of terns were fishing, skimming close to the surface, their handsome black heads alert for minnows or any other food. Farther out, a few gulls swam like ducks on the blue water among a scattering of green-and-white lobster buoys.

Polly waved her hand in a sweeping gesture. "Did I tell you Dr. Summers's remark about the seashores of New England?"

"No. Tell me."

"Like the sidewalks of New York, buoys and gulls together."

Tom said, laughing, that it was a very good pun. Polly laughed, too, but when he turned his head he found her watching him almost solemnly.

"You don't like him, do you?"

"I don't know him at all. A minute or so when we met the ferry. A view of his majestic head smoking a cigar in his garden this morning. How could I judge? But you keep saying he's a wonderful man. So he must be a wonderful man."

Polly's voice was faintly touched with asperity. "How would you describe him, then?"

"A wonderful man."

"No, I mean really."

"You can't say *really*. But that first morning—yesterday morning, when he got off the boat, he seemed upset to find you talking with me."

"How could you ever guess that?"

"He kissed your hand and then made for the car like a pebble out of a sling. He barely acknowledged the introduction."

"That's nothing. That's the way he is. He's very direct. If he has something to do, he goes for it, straight as an arrow."

Tom grinned at her across the worn surface of the rock. "That's like deciding whether to call someone determined or stubborn. If you like the person, he's determined. Otherwise he's stubborn."

"He has a sense of humor."

"The one about gulls and buoys is wit, not humor. The mark of a sharp mind. What else has he got? Old-world urbanity? He kisses hands. An English accent, with just a hint of something continental for spice, like ketchup on a hamburger."

She laughed at that. "You sound—like a jealous lover."

He laughed in turn. "I'm only analyzing character. Or manners. In Germany I met a few academics. Some of them were a shade pompous. Of course it had taken brains to get them where they were in the hierarchy. And a lot of grubby slave-labor when they were young. Same with the English. There are damned few senior professorships. You said he was learned. What's his field?"

Polly was gazing out over the water. "I just don't know, Tom. He works in Widener a lot. Sometimes in the Fogg Museum. Once I got a glimpse inside his brief-case. It was full of notes, but I couldn't see what they were about."

"Were they in English?"

"I couldn't see. I suppose they were. He speaks English beautifully. He's a real scholar."

"Has he done any books? Or learned articles? That's what pages of notes usually lead to."

"He never showed me any. Once or twice he mentioned the Fogg, and I used to be there a lot, but he never said what he was doing there."

"What were *you* doing in the Fogg?"

"I worked there part-time in my last two years."

"What last two years?"

"At Radcliffe. Didn't I tell you?"

"I never met a Radcliffe girl before."

"A jocund company," said Polly. "Really with it. And none of us has ever seen your paintings."

"The paintings can wait. I'd be ashamed to show them to a girl who had worked in Fogg Museum."

"Then what about the place where it happened?"

"What place?"

"Where you found the man. You promised to show me."

"Come on," he said. He took her hand and led her along the beach to the eastward, toward the spot where he had walked that night that now seemed so long ago. Then he was alone. Now not alone. It was very different. A few hundred yards from the flat rock he stopped, gauging the height of the cliffs overhead. "About here," he said, pensively. "It seems like a thousand years ago." He kicked the sand where he thought the corpse had lain.

"Who was he?" she asked. "Do they know?"

"A boy named Freddy Starr. Just graduated from Harvard. You must have known some Harvards."

"Some. I never heard of a Freddy Starr. I'll write my roommate. Maybe she knew him. She was always around the Yard."

"All right, ask her. But don't say he was murdered. They're keeping it dark."

"Poor Freddy, in the double dark."

"Don't we have a lunch somewhere?"

"Sumptuous. Are you hungry?"

"Just this side of starvation."

"All right. I'll unpack if you'll show me your watercolors for dessert. Will you do that?"

They spread out the lunch on the clean, sun-warmed rock. It was more sumptuous than he had supposed, and she had built the menu on a mound of fried chicken. They ate it slowly and threw the bones into the rising tide. She had brought along a bottle of Chablis and a thermos of coffee. He remembered an old movie in which Grace Kelly and Cary Grant had eaten a picnic of fried chicken, with much witty doubletalk about legs and breasts. When he mentioned it idly, she said that she had not seen the film, and went down to wash her hands at the edge of the water. Coming back, she knelt beside him and dried her hands on a napkin from the basket.

"Now they're not greasy," she said, "and they won't spoil your watercolors. Would you like to finish the Chablis?" She leaned across him to get the bottle, sat back on her heels, and thrust the paper cup into his hand, pouring it full.

"Don't you want any?"

"I'll have coffee," she said, "after dessert." She slid the black portfolio into his lap. "Pictures now."

The knots in the string that held it together were giving him trouble. "They're only sketches," he said. "Don't expect Monet or Michelangelo." He began handing them across to her, one by one.

"Tom, they're good," she said enthusiastically. "Like this one of Cuttyhunk."

"What do you know about Cuttyhunk?" he asked, suddenly.

"It's an island. With an Indian name."

"Yes, but what does it mean? The name itself?"

"Lone pine tree in middle of field in middle of island."

"Is that right?"

"No, Tom," she said, laughing. "I'm only making it up. But that's usually the kind of thing those names mean. Like Agamenticus."

"What is that?"

"It's a little mountain in Maine. In Vermont they'd call it a hill. It's near York Harbor where my mother and I stayed with Letitia for a while after my father died. And they say Agamenticus means an island in the middle of a river."

"But you don't know about Cuttyhunk."

"Oh, Tom. Stop rubbing it in. No, I don't know that. But I do know your paintings are good. I mean really good."

"Pure flattery," said Tom. "Blarney and balderdash."

"No, but aren't you always seeing pictures in museums that make you say you could do better?"

"As a matter of fact, no," said Tom, laughing.

"You're too modest."

"I saw a lot of pictures in German museums that I couldn't dream of matching in a million years."

"Well, yes. But how about that modern American school that does bands of color, just bands of color?"

"They're colorful."

"Or one that's in the Fogg. It's all flat black, except for a tiny white star up in one corner. The title is *Night.* You should hear the sub-sub-curator rave about it."

He stirred on the sun-warmed rock and sat up. The wine had made him sleepy, but it was something else—the feeling of a presence—that made him glance up and down the beach. For as far as he could see in both directions there was no movement except for the waves, higher now, curling and bursting against the shore. He glanced at his watch. Four-fifteen. The skin was prickling on the back of his neck. He shuddered and stood up quickly, stretching his arms and turning.

A tall man, who looked enormous against the background of the quiet sky, had drawn back suddenly from the top of the cliff.

"Don't look now," Tom murmured. "We have a visitor."

She pursed her lips with the one-word question.

"Up there on the cliff," said Tom. "Otto the Great."

Chapter Four

1

SHE HAD promised to come back and pick him up at Cora's house sometime in the afternoon of the second day, and now he sat waiting in the meager sunshine on the steps of the cabin where he had slept for the past two nights. All the day before, under a gray overcast which sometimes threw down spatters of rain, he had searched alongshore from the dunes below the cabins past the cliffs where the body had been hurled over, and on out to the farthest extremity of Gay Head itself, playing a hunch that somewhere he would come on a hiding-place, a cave or a cache, where something might have been hidden away from such prying eyes as his own. But he had found nothing. Not even footprints, he thought bitterly. Both nights he had slept badly, twisting and turning in his sleeping-bag on the squeaking bed in Cora's cabin. This morning's search among the fields and woods, fanning out from the place where the dog Nix had appeared with the severed head, had been as unproductive as the coastline had been the day before.

Somewhere, he thought. Somehow. Some thing. That was almost the sum of it all. There were too many unknowns. What about those noises that Cora had complained of? Were they made by men? Or were they only the sound of nightwind in the eaves, round the corners of the house, or in the branches of nearby trees? What about her report of the parked car flashing its lights out to sea from Moshup's Trail? Was it only her imagination, aroused and made suspicious by such events as the theft of Tom's motorcycle? Were the people in the car adolescents playing a game of some kind? Or did their flashing lights mean something genuinely sinister?

You could not tell from the evidence at hand, he thought, any more than you could be certain of the reason that lay behind the sudden apparition of Otto, the doctor's chauffeur and gardener, high on the cliff above their heads that afternoon of the picnic. These and a hundred other questions had hounded him whenever he was awake during those two restive nights. The nights, luckily, were behind him now. But the questions remained.

A sudden movement among the ferns beyond the cabin made him jump. He stayed without motion, waiting, his eyes fixed on the brown-green clump, for the half-minute before Cora's brindled cat walked slowly out and dropped a dead mouse on the ground. They move like lionesses, thought Tom, with that same tilt of the head and the same deliberate shoulders. The cat's pointed ears, mounted on their ingenious swivels, bent alertly forward and then to either side, like small radars ready to catch any sound. Tom sat perfectly still. The green eyes, with their strange vertical slits, were gazing out over the dappled grass-plot. More than a minute passed before it turned its head in his direction. When it saw him at last the eyes widened, as if in surprise. He stared back and the cat looked away. Then it rose from its haunches, took up the mouse once more, and moved slowly across the grass, each forefoot delicately placed, until it had disappeared, as noiselessly as it had come, into the tall brown weeds.

Animal carrying thing, thought Tom. It would make a good title for a picture. Maybe someone had used it already, the idea if not the title. Some brilliant primitive like Rousseau. But here it was in reality, before your eyes, on a patch of sunlit grass. Painter take note. Like a hint from the presiding powers to abandon seascapes and turn to anatomies. First Nix, carrying head. Now the tabby, mouse in mouth. Beasts of prey. Anatomize that one, he told himself, and see where you come out.

The slamming sound of an automobile door brought him quickly to his feet and around the near corner of Cora's house. Polly was still standing beside the car on the driver's side, groping for something in the depths of her leather handbag.

"Tom," she said brightly. "Any luck?"

He shook his head. She was, he was thinking, a sight for sore eyes, as Cora had said. She was wearing a light suit of Black Watch plaid and waving a sheet of white paper.

"I had some luck," she said. "I found out some more about your Freddy Starr. Here. Read all about it."

"What's this?" he asked stupidly, his eyes on her face.

"It's my typing," she said. "Remember I said I'd write my roommate, Helen, and ask if she'd ever met Freddy Starr. I telephoned her instead. She knew him. At least she'd been in classes with him. So I took notes on what she said and typed them up for you. Read what it says."

"Helen thought everybody around Harvard Square must have known Freddy Starr," Polly had written. "Scion of the Concord Starrs and a real screwball. She says she can still see him sitting in the back row of that lecture-room in Sever, gazing all around him with his beatific brown eyes and the long curling lashes that any girl would envy. Very talented, and knew it. She never saw him do a lick of work, not a lick, but what saved him was his beautiful examinations. He had a habit of coming late to classes, she thought obviously to make an entrance. He had a black coat made of bearskin or dogskin and he'd come in wearing that and eating a banana. The professor, she thinks his name was Hewell, used to look up from his notes and scowl. After a while he began ignoring Freddy. Helen doesn't know what grade Freddy got in the course, but she thinks it was probably an A. He had brown eyes, as said, black curly hair, and a hollow chest. Last year he had a job in Widener, sharking up books for a visiting professor. Helen remembers him checking out whole armfuls at the checker's desk down in the front lobby. End of report."

"That's a fine report," Tom said.

"Wouldn't you say she makes you *see* Freddy?"

"I'm glad to know what he was like alive," said Tom. "Did she ever meet his family?"

"I didn't ask," said Polly. "Should I have found out?"

"No. It doesn't matter. Just curiosity. You wonder—"

"Yes, and you wonder how he got over here, and when, and what he did that made them murder him." She stopped suddenly. "But never mind Freddy. What about you, Tom? You look tired to death."

"An exaggeration," he said, smiling at her expression. "Bored to death is more like it. I did a lot of walking and found out exactly nothing. I saw Cora's cat with a dead mouse. That's as close to murder as I ever got. Please don't look so worried."

She was smiling back at him now, with the perfect teeth and the gray eyes that he had remembered through both the fitful nights. "Well, I am worried," she said. "Do you know a state trooper named Milliken?"

"I'm his deputy," Tom said. "As such I rate a salute."

She saluted him, mock British style, palm out. "He telephoned this morning," she said. "He wants to see you. He didn't know where you were."

"I'll call him. Was it anything important?"

"I told him what you were doing, and that I was going to come and pick you up today. He seemed to be relieved. He wants you to call him but there's no special hurry. He'll either be at the station or at home. I told him I was going to give you a drink and some dinner. Will you come?"

"I'll get my gear," Tom said. "Give me five minutes. Mrs. Pease wants to see you. Since she met you she's hardly talked of anything else."

"She's a doll," Polly said. "A real Wampanoag Indian doll. I'll go call on her. Just throw your stuff in the back of the car, and please remember to bring the watercolors."

"For dessert," said Tom. "Wasn't that it?"

Over her shoulder Polly threw him a wink. "That's it," she said. "Better than any other. No cholesterol."

2

In the car on the way to Edgartown, he asked her about Otto. "Spying on us from the cliff," he said, flatly. "Did you ask him about it?"

"He wasn't spying," said Polly, defensively. "At least not exactly. You know he went over to Falmouth to pick up the Mercedes. It was being fixed. They've had so much trouble with it that when he came back with the car, Dr. Summers suggested that they ought to give it a trial run. He called it a little spin."

"Who told you that?"

"Dr. Summers."

"So the little spin took them, of all places, all the way out to Gay Head. Was that it?"

"That's as far as you can go on this island, Tom."

"Did they know you were there?"

"Dr. Summers said they didn't. But when they drove up by the lighthouse, they saw my car. It was locked and empty. Dr. Summers said they were worried."

"Worried about what?"

"Oh, he apologized. He said that young girls weren't safe these days if they were out alone."

"Even on the Vineyard?"

"Even on the Vineyard, yes. Seeing the empty car worried him. So he sent Otto out to look for me. Otto saw us from a great distance down on the beach, on that flat rock. Dr. Summers asked if he was sure it was me. Otto said it was too far away to be certain. So they drove down Moshup's Trail and Otto parked beside the road and went over to the edge and looked down and there we were."

"And that was when I had the chill and looked up and saw him," said Tom. "And where was Summers all this time?"

"Waiting in the car. He just wanted to be sure I was all right."

"So he sent Otto to spy on us."

"Just checking. Isn't that your favorite verb—checking?"

"One of them," said Tom. "Do you believe that story?"

Polly braked the car to avoid a rabbit. "You know, Tom," she said, "we're never so close to quarreling as when we're talking about Dr. Summers."

"And his muscle-man, Otto. Who gave them the right to check on your every move?"

"Not *every* move, Tom. This was just a special case. You still sound like a jealous lover."

"Put it the other way. What about him? A man of sixty!"

"He never made a pass at me, if that's what you mean," said Polly sharply. "And he was very apologetic about this."

"He'd better be."

"There you go. He felt so apologetic he lent me the keys to his house again and invited me to use the piano."

"While he's there? You said—"

"Oh, no, he's gone away. He and Otto left in the Mercedes this morning."

"Left? For where?"

"He didn't say. Maybe Harvard. Sometimes they go to New Haven. To work at Yale."

"A real scholar," said Tom.

"Oh, Tom, stop it." She pointed the car into Water Street and slowed for the turn into the driveway of her aunt's house. "Come on in and have a drink. After dinner I'll show you the Summers mansion. It's worth a visit."

The screen door slammed behind them like the crack of a rifle. In the hall she turned suddenly, seized his ears lightly in her cool hands, and kissed him fully on the mouth. "That's for you," she said. "This is for me." And kissed him again, lingeringly.

His arms were around her slender waist, drawing her close. "There's some name for it," he said. "Like electricity."

"I thought of that," she said. "The first time you came through that door I thought just that. You turn me on. What do they call it? Alternating current?"

"Direct current."

79

She was drawing away gently. "It's dangerous," she said. "People have been known to be electrocuted. How about a drink?"

"After that I don't need a drink."

"Have one anyway, and fix me one while I heat up the dinner. The liquor's here in the pantry. I'll have a gin and tonic. A gill of gin and a lot of tonic. You have what you like. We're going to eat in the kitchen."

"The formerly medieval kitchen. With the view of Dr. Summers's garden."

She was setting the controls on the electric stove. "Except that it's too dark now to see the flowers. And you wouldn't like them, anyway."

"Why not?"

"Dr. Summers raised them," said Polly, laughing. When she came over to claim her drink, she kissed him lightly once again. "That's just to show you whose side I'm on," she said.

When she had unlocked the massive front door, he saw that the large room beyond it was full of shadows, invaded only dimly by the light from the hall and the far-off glow of the streetlight. She pressed the switch beside the door and half a dozen reading-lamps flashed on at once, each disposed beside a comfortable deep chair. The room was octagonal, with books from floor to ceiling on every wall except the one where the huge fireplace yawned. Some of the books were in leatherbound sets, as Tom saw, idly browsing: Dickens, Twain, Tolstoy, Goethe.

"Are all these his, or did they come with the house?"

"I don't know," said Polly. "He moved in before my time. Letitia says—"

"How long ago?"

"A long time ago. Letitia says he had workmen here for at least six months. She was glad when the mess was cleaned up. I don't know. Maybe five or six years after the war."

"Does he read all these books?"

"I don't know him that well," Polly said. "But he must read a lot. His light is on late every night whenever he's here. But I think he's really a scholar."

"What's the difference between a scholar and a reader?"

"A reader reads," said Polly, crisply. "A scholar looks things up."

Tom was standing before a shelf of massive tomes, reading off the titles. "Like Christian art and iconology," he said. "Here's a dictionary of Christian antiquities. And one Stammler, *Le Trésor de la Cathédrale de Lausanne*. And another on the Russian ikon. Is that what he studies at Harvard and Yale?"

"It could be," said Polly, carelessly. She had gone to sit on the mahogany piano bench. "He never talks about it."

"Maybe he's studying autobiographies," said Tom. "Here's a Cellini, bound up in red leather, no doubt by a Florentine craftsman. John Gower, *Confessio Amantis*. The *Confessions* of St. Augustine."

But Polly did not seem to be listening. She had opened the piano and her hands were moving silently over the keys.

"Never mind the books," said Tom. "Play me a piece." He sat down in one of the deep chairs, admiring her profile as she sat erect on the piano bench, turning the pages of music on the rack.

"I'm afraid I'd flub it. I'm too excited."

"No, you won't. Try it anyhow."

"What would you like?"

"What have you been working on?"

"I've been trying to play *Für Elise* like Artur Schnabel."

"Play it like Polly Harmon."

She found the piece and bent forward while her long fingers lightly and swiftly moved through the tinkle of the opening bars. When it was over and her hands were again in her lap, she turned half round to him, her eyes alight.

"It was lovely," he said. "Schnabel never did it better."

"It's a wonderful piano. It does half the work."

Tom got up from his chair and crossed the room to her side, sauntering leisurely, with no appearance of haste. His hands touched her shoulders as she sat on the bench, and he leaned forward to kiss the side of her neck.

"Thank you," she said. "That's almost like the piano ad."

But he was whispering into her ear. "Polly, pretend I'm only kissing you. Nod or shake your head. Is there anyone in this house?"

She shook her head, her gray eyes wide.

"There was someone in the hall, the back hall behind my chair. Don't look now, but are you sure they went away this morning?"

She nodded, and turned her head to kiss his cheek. "I know they went," she whispered. "I was in Oak Bluffs and saw them drive aboard the ferry around ten."

"Keep kissing me," said Tom. "What were you doing in Oak Bluffs?"

Polly's lips were still against his cheek. "Buying your dinner, silly," she whispered. "What makes you think there's someone here?"

He lifted her chin gently and kissed her mouth. "A noise in that hall. Very faint but it made me look around. The door was being closed."

Polly was gazing across the room. "The door's open," she said in a soft voice.

"Part way open," he whispered. "It was moving when I looked."

"Maybe the wind."

"There is no wind."

"Or your imagination."

"Imagination inactive," he said quietly. "No, Polly, someone's in this house."

3

"If it was ever anybody," said Polly, "they're gone now, wouldn't you say?" Her voice was still so low that it was barely audible. "And they wouldn't know we know, because they'd think we were only kissing."

Tom's lean jaw was set. "Maybe gone, maybe not. Look, Polly, let's try something. I'll go back and sit down and you play again. Something loud. Like Beethoven."

She nodded. "Go sit down, lover," she said in a normal voice, "and I'll play you another."

He waited for only a moment while the great chords crashed in the room and then swung up slowly, flattened his back against the bookshelves, and moved sideways to the door until, with a sudden lunge, he pushed it wide open and stepped back out of range. It swung back unimpeded. Even through the sound of the music he could hear it bang against the wall of the dark corridor that lay behind it. He caught Polly's eye and shook his head. The light from the living-room showed a brown door at the end of the passage. It was closed and the corridor was empty.

He motioned to Polly to go on playing, moved silently to the farther door, and turned the handle. It was locked, apparently from the other side, since there was no keyhole. He knelt for a moment on the carpet, with both hands close to the doorsill, before returning to the lighted room, closing the near door to its former position, and sitting down beside Polly on the piano-bench.

"You can stop now," he said. "Nobody's there. What does that far door lead to?"

She was watching him quizzically. "I don't know. I never went out that way. Do you still think there was someone there?"

"Even more so. That far door is tight. There's not a breath of a draft around the sill. Certainly not enough to move this inside door. And I saw it moving."

She was watching him gravely. "I believe you, Tom, but—"

"But you think it's impossible. Who are the people of this house?"

"Dr. Summers and Otto."

"No others? Not even—er—transients?"

"None that I ever saw. But of course I don't keep a watch. It never occurred to me to keep a watch."

He was silent beside her. "No, of course you wouldn't keep a watch, except as one neighbor to another. Still, you know when they've gone away."

"Usually," she said. "Not always."

"Maybe Milliken could arrange one," he said musingly.

"Arrange what?"

"A watch on the house. To see who comes and goes. There must be a door on the harbor side."

"Oh, yes. There are at least two. And then the boathouse."

"What about the boathouse?"

"He has a very elaborate one with a sort of—a sort of little canal that leads into it from the tidal channel."

"How do you know? Have you been there?"

"No, but you can see it from the harbor. Like a double garage, with his sailboat on one side and the motorboat on the other. And those pull-up doors."

"Milliken would have his hands full, setting up a watch," said Tom.

"You forgot about calling him."

"I didn't forget. I just postponed the call for the dinner hour and the musicale."

"Hadn't you better call him now?"

"Maybe I'd better."

He pulled up on the sandy loam before Milliken's bungalow, set the parking-stand, untied his luggage from the rack, and carried it up across the porch to the front door, which was standing open.

"That you, Tom?" said Milliken's voice from the kitchen. "Come on out here. How about some coffee?"

"Thanks, I will. You're working late."

There was an untidy pile of typed sheets on the table, along with an empty coffee-cup and a well-chewed cigar butt in the saucer. He got up briskly, found another cup, and filled it from the electric percolator. "How do you want it?"

"Black is fine, thanks. What are you doing?"

Milliken stretched, flexing the muscles of his powerful sloping shoulders. "That thing is a copy of the lab report on our friend Freddy Starr."

"What's the use? He's dead."

"Oh, it's useful enough. They found out a few things."

"Such as what?"

"Time of death, for one thing," said Milliken. "It says here he was probably killed in the early morning of the night you found him. Rigor mortis was still evident when we picked him up. Remember those arms?"

Tom nodded.

"In these latitudes at this season the rigor lasts for around twenty-four to twenty-six hours. So that enters in. They also say the—er—chopping was done with an ax that had been used on pine trees. Seems they found some fragments of pine pitch on the skin at the base of the neck."

"I wouldn't be too sure about that," said Tom. "That big black dog Nix was carrying the head through a grove of pines when I made him drop it."

"I thought they said it was on the trunk, not the head," said Milliken. "Here, let me see. The damn thing is all in medical language." He ran a stained finger down the lines of typing, turned a page, read further, then suddenly gave it up. "I can't see it now, but I do recall they mentioned pine-needle fragments in the hair. They've also got a reading on the clown face."

"The gay head."

"I mean the red markings. They say it was done with lipstick."

"A woman in the case?"

Milliken made a negative gesture. "Anybody can buy a lipstick. They think the ax and the pitch both point to murder in the woods. There are plenty of woods on the island, and the job could have been done in any of them. Or somewhere else, for that matter."

"You mean on the mainland?"

"Could be. Not likely, but it could have been. All we know is that the body and the head were carried away from the site of the murder. And here's something else. They determined the menu of Freddy's last meal: a hamburger, some milk, and an apple."

"Does that help?"

"Perhaps a little. He could have picked up an apple in any orchard and bought the milk in any store. But the hamburger had to be cooked by someone. In October there's a limit to the number of places on the island where you can buy a hamburger. Harry Royce is checking."

"Suppose he was a prisoner before they killed him," said Tom.

"I thought of that. You mean they wouldn't be likely to feed him if they were planning to kill him."

"That's one possible guess. Do they know how he was killed?"

"They say the medical evidence points to strangulation. Then decapitation, or so they call it here. Finally—er—decoration, or however you want to describe what they did. They say he might have been beaten up first. Two of the ribs were broken, on the left side."

"That could have happened in the fall down the cliff."

Milliken pursed his lips and narrowed his eyes. "It could have," he said musingly. His thick eyebrows were set in a frown. "Either way, it makes me kind of sick, doesn't it you? You see stuff like that in a war. That or worse. But it doesn't fit our landscape."

4

Milliken was more than skeptical about setting a watch on the Summers house. First, he said, there was the problem of economics. The only way to run a watch like that was around the clock. That would require the services of at least two men. There was no money to pay for *one*, let alone two or three. And anyway, what would be the purpose? To see who went in and out? The answer to that was known already: Dr. Summers and chauffeur. Maybe a delivery boy with the groceries once or twice a week. You couldn't pay a couple of people for that kind of information.

Take another angle. What had Summers done to deserve being watched? He and his silent servant drove around in the Mercedes. Separately or together, with or without the car, they occasionally crossed to Woods Hole on the ferry. Sometimes Dr. Summers was driven to the airport and took one of the Executive planes to Boston. Sometimes the other man went along, sometimes not. What they did had to be their business. At home he lived quietly. He neither disturbed the peace nor threw noisy parties nor seduced the island virgins, assuming that there were some. Even his speedboat ran as smoothly and almost as silently as clockwork. There was not one damn thing you could pin on him or accuse him of that would warrant a cordon of observers around his mansion.

About that moving door. The girl—what was her name? Polly Harmon. How long had she been living there in the neighboring house? Since June. All right, take the middle of June to the middle of October—four months. If anyone else was living in the Summers place, a smart girl like that would have found it out in four months' time. Or would she?

Milliken threw the question carelessly at Tom, who shrugged.

Yet still, he said stubbornly, that damn door had moved.

"Let's go over it," Milliken said. "If it moved, it was not moved by any draft from the end of the corridor because you checked, and at the time you checked there was no evidence of a draft, right? What about a draft from the front door?"

No, Tom said flatly. The moving door was hung the other way. A draft from the front door, which had probably been closed anyway, would have blown it open. Instead, from the extreme right corner of his right eye, he had seen it being slowly closed.

"Closed?"

"Well, almost closed."

"Closed enough, you mean, so that anyone behind it could have tiptoed down the corridor under the cover of Polly's music and got out through the farther door, closing and locking it behind him?"

Tom nodded. "Yes, assuming it was a man. It might have been a woman."

Milliken exploded in an incredulous laugh. "Now how the hell—what made you say that? A woman! Why a woman?"

Tom felt the flush, half anger and half shame, climbing his neck and suffusing his cheeks. "Summers could have a wife," he said belligerently.

Milliken was still laughing. "A crazy wife that he keeps locked up? A deformed wife who won't show her face? Come on, Tom, I've seen some movies, too. What have you got against Summers, anyway?"

Tom's jaw was set. "Nothing but a moving door, Lieutenant," he said evenly. "Nothing but a moving door in a house that was supposed to be empty."

Milliken's laughter rumbled to rest in his throat and his heavy eyebrows came together in a frown. For a full minute he said nothing. Almost automatically his fingers gathered up the sheets of the lab report on Freddy Starr and arranged them in a neat pile.

"To a cop," he said at last, "it could mean break-and-enter. The owner's away, we don't know where. He hasn't lodged any complaint. We have no jurisdiction. We have no search warrant. We could call the Edgartown chief and have him investigate. But we don't know for sure that anyone's in the house."

"Polly has the key," said Tom quickly. "She's authorized to enter."

"Why?"

"To use the piano. What time is it? My watch has stopped."

Milliken pointed to the electric clock on the wall behind the desk. It showed nine-forty-five.

"It's not too late," said Tom. "I'll call her and go back there to Edgartown."

"Be my guest," Milliken said. It was a phrase Tom hated, but he ignored it and picked up the phone.

She met him at the front door and slipped the key into his hand. "Are you sure you won't let me come?"

"I'd better do it alone. Milliken thinks it might be a burglar. If it is—or was—we probably scared him away. Otherwise—"

"If he's still there and you catch him, Dr. Summers will

be grateful. If he's gone, *I'll* be grateful. Please be careful, Tom."

"I'll be careful."

On the way up the long front walk he kept to the shadows of the tree-trunks. A few dry leaves rustled under his feet. The gun was in the right side pocket of his jacket and he carried the flashlight in his other hand. At the top of the granite steps he unlocked the door, pushed it slowly part way open, and stepped inside. The hall and the octagonal room behind it were faintly illuminated by the distant street-light. He closed the door silently and waited, holding his breath.

No sound. His canvas shoes whispered against the carpeting as he moved into the book-lined room beyond. He stood with his back to a shelf of books in the darkest place he could find and waited again, listening. There was no sound except that of his own breathing. The door to the back corridor stood open but he could not see through to the brown door at the far end. He stepped quickly into and along the corridor, shifted the flashlight to his right hand, and thumbed it on. The brown door was closed.

In two strides he was beside it, his hand on the brass knob. It clicked once as he turned it and pushed. The door swung open and he slipped through into the absolute darkness of the room beyond it.

But it was not a room. His outstretched arms touched the walls on either side. It was another corridor, narrower than the first. Again he stood listening; again he flashed the light, held it on for the count of five, and snapped it off. This time there were two doors, one at the end, the other halfway down on the right. The far one was locked with a Yale lock, and the bottom edge was weather-stripped. Obviously the back door, he thought, leading out perhaps to or into the boathouse. He turned to the door on the right of the hallway and tried the knob. This one was also locked, but from the far side. He bent to the old-fashioned keyhole and flashed on his light. There was a key in the keyhole. He knelt to it, laid his ear against it, and caught his breath. The sound of music, very faint but unmistakable, was coming from somewhere beyond the door. He lay full-length on the carpet and brought his right ear close to the crack beneath the door. The music stopped and he heard the far gabble of a human voice. After a minute the voice ceased and the music began again.

Tom got to his knees and stood up. There could be no question. Someone in a distant room beyond this door in Summers's cavernous mansion was listening to a radio or watching television.

But who? Summers and Otto had driven aboard the *Islander* at ten o'clock that morning. They would hardly have come back so soon. The house was locked and no lights were burning. There was no evidence of any burglary, actual or attempted—no windows open, no broken glass, no drawers pulled out and contents scattered, nothing unlocked that should be locked. Only the faint sound of music from the other side of a door.

He stood irresolute in the darkness. So what do we do now? he thought. The music means that someone's in the house, and the presence of someone accounts for what I saw some time ago, the silently closing door of the living-room. Whoever it was heard Polly's playing and came up to check. He (or she) saw me there, closed the door to the hall, went along through the brown door, locking it behind him (or her), and came back into this part of the house.

The luminous dial of his wristwatch showed that it was a

few minutes past eleven. It had been close to seven when he had listened to Polly's playing. The house had been quiet for a long time. The watchman, if that was who he was, would be feeling secure. Perhaps he was in bed. So, Tom thought again, what do we do? Do we go on back through the house and out the front door and hand the key to Polly and go make a report to Milliken? Or do we try to find out who this nameless character is?

Naming the alternatives, he found, was enough. He thrust the flashlight into his lefthand pocket, moved quickly to the back door, unlatched and set the lock, and stepped out into the cold night air.

5

Out there, at least, there was enough light to see by. Stars were looking down. He was standing in a sort of compound, thirty or forty feet square, with high brick walls from which the whitewash was peeling. There were a couple of small flowerbeds, arranged to catch the sun. All the rest of the area was paved with brick. The wall towards the water was broken by the rear elevation of what must be the boathouse, the door to it heavily barred with strips of iron. He lifted his eyes to the top of the wall. Silhouetted against the night sky he could see tangled strands of barbed wire.

"Whew," he exclaimed, half aloud. "A regular fortress."

Against the white wall of the house to his left was stacked some garden furniture, four or five chairs and a table ready to be taken inside for the winter. To his right was one of those flat sunbathing couches, made of webbing stretched over a light aluminum frame. This must be the place where the eminent scholar came to take his airings and his tannings, away from prying eyes. Or maybe it was Otto who laid his torso there, flexing his giant muscles in the morning sun.

It was then that Tom saw the pair of two-foot windows, their sills nearly flush with the brick pavement, that had been let into the back wall of the house. There was an interval between them that made them seem like blind eyes staring out into the walled yard. Carefully skirting the sunbathing couch, he moved closer and went down on one knee to peer into the nearer of the two windows. But the glass was opaque, blacked out from inside with a layer of dark paint. Still moving carefully, he went to the far window. This, too, was painted over except for a point of light like an irregular star far down in one corner—a spot that the painter had missed, or where a small blob of paint had flaked off. He leaned down to peer in, but there was nothing much to see. Only what might be the worn edge of a work-table or bench, streaked with what looked like stains of old paint. He leaned as far as he could in the other direction. Hanging above the rough table was the source of illumination, a bare electric bulb. From somewhere in the room behind it he heard, less faintly than from the hallway above, the steady blather of a radio announcer's voice.

So here it was: the basement retreat of the nameless night watchman, or whoever it was that had climbed the stairs, entered the back hall, opened the brown door, and made his silent way along the corridor until he could lean forward far enough to see Tom Cook sitting in the deep chair in the octagonal library, listening to Polly Harmon's music. Both

Polly and afterwards Milliken had been dubious about Tom's account of the slowly closing door. But this, he thought triumphantly, was clear proof that it had happened, that the door had actually moved, that he had not, after all, been seeing things that were not there, that had not happened.

Or was it no proof at all? Squatting there on his heels in the semi-darkness beside the chink of light in the painted window, knowing that inside the basement room was a workbench with a stark bulb above it and somewhere nearby a radio emitting the customary sounds, what did that prove? It could be that Otto, repairing something in the basement room, had merely forgotten to turn off the light and the radio before he left with Dr. Summers in the Mercedes.

He stiffened with a sudden leap of fear at the grip of a hand on his shoulder and another hand that covered his mouth—and found himself looking up in astonishment into Polly's face. Her hand left his shoulder and she laid her index finger across her lips. He nodded and she took the other hand away, only to cup his elbow and help him to stand. Her lips were close to his ear now.

"Come away," she breathed.

He pointed to the star-spot of light on the painted window. She nodded briskly but pulled him into the shadows of the wall on the other side of the compound. She was wearing sneakers and blue jeans and a dark sweater.

"How'd you get in here?" he whispered.

She was smiling at him in the faint starlight. "Over the wall," she said softly. "With a step-ladder on the garden side. In among the bushes."

He gestured at the top of the wall. "All that barbed wire—"

"Tore my britches," she said in silent laughter. "But the worst was the jump down. It's high from up there. I hung down and dropped. Then I saw a man squatting down beside the house." Her finger touched his shoulder, pointing. "The man was you."

"Let's get out of here," said Tom.

"Over the wall?"

He shook his head vigorously. "No. Out through the house."

"But what about *him?*"

"Never mind him. Come on. Let's go."

He did not breathe easily until he had led her through the front hall and out to the granite steps, where he closed and locked the door and handed her the key. "Now let's go get that step-ladder," he said. "Is it yours or his?"

"His," said Polly. "Otto was using it to trim the top of the hedge."

"Careless Otto."

"Why careless?"

"He left it out and a lady burglar used it."

"And tore her pants on his damned barbwire," said Polly.

"You shouldn't have come."

"I couldn't stand not to. You disappeared. I checked your motorcycle. It was still there. You hadn't ridden away on it. I checked the front door of the Summers place. It was locked. There wasn't a light in the house—"

"Except in the basement," said Tom. "Where did you find this stepladder?"

"Over here beside the hedge. No, not there. Right here."

"Good," said Tom, lowering it to the ground. "Back where it came from." He went close to her, a hand on each of her shoulders, and looked into her face. "Now who was right about the moving door?"

She was chuckling. "I don't know. What did you find?"

He told her.

Her face was serious now. "I don't know who it could be."

"It might have been Otto, working in the basement, leaving the light and the radio on. Forgetting them. Going off with Summers."

She was frowning. "But that wouldn't account for the moving door, would it?"

"No. Did you ever see anyone else around the place? Any visitors? Any workmen?"

Polly shook her head. Suddenly she was shivering. "It's cold out here, Tom. Aren't you cold?"

"Maybe a nervous reaction," he said. "After all your hedge-hopping."

"Wall-climbing," she said between chattering teeth. "Pants-tearing. Oh, Tom, I'm cold. Let's go inside."

"It's late. Your neighbors will talk. They'll hear my midnight motorcycle going away and your reputation will be ruined."

"Never mmmind," she said, shivering. "Come on in. I b-built us a fire. Oh, and Milliken called. He wants you to call him back. He's at home. If anybody comes to the door we can be roasting some mmmarshmallows."

Chapter Five

1

MILLIKEN'S VOICE, hoarse on the telephone, rasped out a proposition: Tom, and maybe Polly, to fly to Boston in the morning to find out whatever they could about Freddy Starr's activities in Cambridge. Polly's former roommate might help.

"You got her report," said Tom.

"I read the report, yes. But, Tom, I've been in this business long enough to know there's no substitute for nosing around on the ground."

"Like a bird dog," said Tom. "If we both go, it'll leave the house next door uncovered."

"Royce can keep an eye on the house. After all, Tom, we've still got this murder on our hands. It's more than a week now. A little bird-dogging in Cambridge . . ."

"Hold on. I'll ask Polly." Tom put the phone down and explained. Milliken would book them on the nine o'clock plane. "Will you go with me? What about your friend Helen? Could she help us? Is it too late to call her tonight?"

Polly sat up straight in the chair. "Yes, yes, yes, and yes," she said. "Helen's a night-owl, or used to be. That's no problem. I'll call her right away."

The light plane rose smoothly in the gray morning. Fog

lay in swaths along the green and brown coast. They came down at Logan with a bump, took the train to Harvard Square, and emerged into light rain. Polly tied the shiny red rain-hat over her dark hair and under her chin and chattered about Radcliffe while they walked through the Yard past the majestic marble of the Widener steps. They had come between classes. Men and women streamed along the walks and across the sere October grass. The windows of Lamont looked grimy and the air inside was hazy with smoke. Students slouched barefoot in the chairs among the shelves, open books in their laps. One boy was asleep, his loafers, roughly repaired with strips of adhesive tape, tumbled beside his chair.

Helen Mahoney waved at them from the circulation desk—a plain-featured redhead with freckles across the bridge of her nose. She hugged Polly and shook hands with Tom. "I haven't had time to look up the circulation records," she said. "They're over back. Let me check out this book and we'll see." She stamped the date in a tome for one of the students and led the way to a tall file where she riffled through the cards. "It's just as I thought," she said, frowning. "There's absolutely nothing here. Freddy must have worked in Widener. Let me give Alice Colman a call."

They arranged to meet Helen for lunch and climbed the Widener steps. Polly knew the checker at the gate, a middle-aged man named Camparotta, his oiled hair combed neatly and thinly over the dome of his skull.

"Long time no see," Camparotta said. "How you been keeping yourself? You looking good."

"Fine," said Polly. "This is Tom Cook. We're looking for information about a boy named Freddy Starr. Do you remember Freddy Starr?"

Mr. Camparotta gently struck his forehead with the heel

of his hand and rolled his brown eyes. "He's gone, thang God. Graduated. Not here this fall."

"What was wrong with Freddy?" asked Tom.

With his right forefinger Mr. Camparotta described small circles beside his right ear. "Nuts," he said. "That boy was nuts. Also, too much money. Also too much dope. At one time, you understand. He comes in here riding a cloud, you know what I mean?" Mr. Camparotta spread his hands. "What you gonna do? They take hold of him, cure him up. He's a smart enough boy, just nutty. So he graduates."

"We think he had a job last spring," Polly said. "Working for a visiting professor. Do you remember that?"

Mr. Camparotta smiled and spread his hands again. "Here is Grand Central Station," he said. "I remember the boy. About the professor I wouldn't know. We just make sure the books were charged out upstairs."

"Thank you, Mr. Camparotta," said Polly, briskly. "We'll go up now." She took Tom's arm and they climbed the stairs under the khaki murals. Alice Colman was a tired-looking black girl who guided them back to the circulation files and quickly explained the system. "I'm supposed to do it myself, but we're short-handed today. I'll be out front if you need me."

Tom flipped through the cards in the S-file. Stagg, Staley, Starr. "Here we are," he said. "Not much here. Let's see."

The titles that Freddy had borrowed, he presently saw, made a kind of pattern. George Roth, *Guide to Early Christian Antiquities*. E. Jusserot, *Les trésors d'art religieux du San Vitale*. Another Frenchman, Jacques d'Alton, had done *Le collane bizantine del Museo di Casablanca*.

"All nations," he said to Polly. "Here's one by a Dutchman, P. van der Meer. *Les trésors des eglises de l'arrondissement de Goffe*."

"What's Goffe?" asked Polly. "I never heard of Goffe."

"I don't know," said Tom. "But the pattern is Christian art, religious art. There's even one here about the jewel-encrusted treasures in the Vatican."

"Innocent enough," said Polly uncertainly. "One of the legitimate departments of learning."

"But an odd subject for a boy like Freddy Starr, wouldn't you think? I'd like to know about that visiting professor that Helen mentioned. Maybe Alice Colman would know."

He came back shaking his head. "No luck," he said. "Alice is new here. Let's copy the names of these books and then go. What time is it, anyway?"

"Nearly lunch-time," said Polly. "Helen has to eat at noon. Here, you read them out and I'll write them down."

Afterwards they thanked Alice Colman and turned to go. Over in the northwest corner an undergraduate and his girl sat forehead to forehead, murmuring in low tones and sharing something from a paper bag.

Tom motioned towards them. "How would you describe that scene?"

"Touching," whispered Polly, giggling. "Literally touching. Like Eliot's lovers, quietly sweating, dome to dome."

They were halfway down the stairs when Tom seized her elbow. "Wait a minute," he said. "I skipped a beat."

"How?"

"Back in that S-file. We only looked at the cards for Freddy Starr. What about Summers? Doesn't he work here, too?"

"Yes, and at Brown and at Yale."

"Let me go back and check," said Tom. "It'll only take a minute."

"I'll go to the ladies' room, and meet you here."

In ten minutes he was back at her side.

"Your eyes are shining," she said. "Any luck?"

"A little. Enough to guess that the visiting professor Freddy worked for might possibly have been Summers. Last spring, on his own, Summers borrowed a book on the religious art of Rouen Cathedral, and in August he spent one day with that one by Jusserot on the art treasures of San Vitale. The same that Freddy took out last winter. Through the summer there were five or six others. I wrote them down. In a way, it proves nothing, except when you think that Freddy Starr might just possibly have been the runner-boy for your Doctor Summers."

"Not mine," said Polly. "I don't claim him."

Tom grinned. "I meant only as a neighbor. Freddy disappeared after commencement. He was murdered on the Vineyard."

"Three months later," said Polly.

"Sure, there are gaps of time. But wouldn't you say that the chances are the Vineyard was the place Freddy chose to disappear into, that he stayed around the island all summer?"

"You don't know that."

"No, we don't know that. Perhaps he came and left and came again. And left finally—in two pieces."

"Ugh," said Polly. "That's not luncheon-talk."

2

Before they left Cambridge for the return flight, Tom telephoned the Starr house in Concord. A sour-voiced domestic said that the Starrs were out of town, time of return uncertain.

Outside the booth he took Polly's arm. "Gone away," he said. "Location not stated. I don't blame them. They must have buried Freddy last week and then took off. Talking to them probably wouldn't have helped. They hadn't even seen him since commencement. This was a hunch that didn't work."

"The other one did," said Polly, "and you can't expect two to work in one day. You proved that Freddy was student assistant for Dr. Summers."

"More or less. It's a lot of trouble for a bag of peanuts."

"Not too much trouble," Polly said. "And I wouldn't call it peanuts. It was a good lunch and you met Helen and now we've flown together for the first time. Second time coming up."

Over the Vineyard airport he took her hand and held it while the small plane circled and descended like a mechanical moth. After they had walked clear of the oily runway, the air smelled pleasantly of pine needles and faintly of the sea.

"Now where?" she said from the other side of the car.

"Are you tired?"

"Not very."

"Let's go report to Milliken."

"We'll do that," she said, turning on the engine and the headlights. Dusk was falling over the fields and woods and the closed-up cottages along Barnes Road past the Lagoon. By Oak Bluffs it was full dark.

"Come in," he said. "This won't take long. Afterwards we can eat at the Seagull."

"All right. Good idea. Under the fishy eye of Ma Pierce. Have you met Ma Pierce?"

"Small woman with a voice like a foghorn."

"That's Ma. And a sailor's vocabulary."

"That's Ma Pierce," he said, laughing.

Inside the office the short wave crackled as always and the light shone over the partition, but the chair by the desk was empty.

"He may be at the Seagull," said Tom. "Let's go see."

As he held open the door for her to pass, they met Harry Royce coming up the station steps. Tom introduced him to Polly, but Harry only nodded curtly. His face was taut and his manner was businesslike. "Looking for Milliken?" he said in his high-pitched voice. "He ain't here. Been Up Island all day."

"Why there?"

"We got trouble," Royce said.

"What kind of trouble?"

Royce glanced at Polly and back at Tom. His lips were set in a thin line and he kept them closed.

"It's all right," said Tom. "She knows everything I know. We just got back from Boston on Milliken's assignment. You said trouble."

"Bad trouble," Royce said. "We got us another murder."

Tom's heart jumped. "Not Cora Pease?"

"Not yet," said Royce sardonically. "Man name of Hupp. You know him. Monty Hupp."

"Dead?"

"Dead."

Tom gripped the edge of the counter and his eyes sought out Polly's. In the harsh light of the station her face was pale. "When did it happen?"

"Sometime last night," Royce said.

"Do they know where?"

"Sure they know. Monty was out on patrol with another man, name of Whitehead. Another patrol boat found theirs grounded on No Man's Land around nine this morning. Whitehead ain't dead but he's shot bad. They got him in the hospital. They don't think he'll make it."

"What about Monty?"

"Took a tommy-gun burst right between the shoulder-blades."

Tom swallowed with an effort. "Where's Milliken now?"

"Fifteen minutes ago he was still at Menemsha."

"Did he say he was coming back?"

"Didn't say. I doubt it. I'm covering here."

Tom turned to Polly. "Could we go home and get my motorcycle? I'll have to go out there."

"I'll drive you out."

"I'd rather you didn't. It might be—"

"Dangerous?" she asked, her eyes wide and dark.

"I didn't mean that. But I'd rather have you home. I want to see if Cora's all right, and I'll call you when I find out anything more. Are you hungry?"

She shook her head. "Should we go?"

He nodded, waving once at Royce. "We'll keep in touch," he said, going out.

There were no stars. A damp wind was blowing in from Nantucket Sound and they could hear the breakers booming along the shore. Polly hunched her shoulders and turned up the collar of her raincoat.

In the car she said: "That's terrible about Monty Hupp. How well did you know him?"

"Not well. Only enough to know he was a good man, and any good man dead is a loss. It'll be rough on his wife."

A dam inside Polly broke suddenly in a rush of words. "Any time a man dies it's rough on his wife. She has to cope. Even what she was coping with before takes on a different dimension. It was that way with my mother and she wilted under it. Letitia did better. She always had more money and more confidence. Now she travels and then stays put and then travels some more. I don't really think she liked Sanford much. But still she had to cope."

"Sanford?"

"Her late husband. A big bluff man with a red face. Died playing golf."

"Margy liked her man."

"Margy?"

"Monty Hupp's wife. Widow now."

"After a while they seem to get along all right," said Polly. "Not that I've made a study of it. But the other day I saw a whole busload of biddies just off the boat at Vineyard Haven. They were on one of those Paragon Tours. You know how they look. Mostly old or on the verge of it, in all the different shapes and sizes, all wearing sensible shoes and with their pink scalps showing through their blue hair. Poor things. I'll bet more than half of them were widows. But they seemed to be having fun."

As she turned into the driveway of Letitia's house, Tom glanced at the house next door. Lights were burning in the octagonal room.

"Where do they keep the Mercedes?"

"In the garage at night."

"There's a light in the library. Does that mean they're home?"

"Probably, but you can't tell."

"I'd still like to find out about that door that moved while you were playing. And that light in the basement where the radio was. Right now I'd like to check that basement for another reason."

"What?"

"Because young Freddy Starr might have spent some time there."

"What makes you think so?"

"If he worked for Summers in Cambridge, he could have worked for Summers here."

"That's impossible. I would have seen him around the place."

"Could you make that remotely possible? After today it doesn't even seem quite so remote."

"It still does to me," said Polly.

Tom saw the old argument coming and chose to avoid it. "I'd like to check that basement anyhow, but I can't as long as the old boy's in residence. Now I'd better wheel out the bike and get out to Menemsha. I'll sleep at Milliken's. If it's not too late, I'll call you from there."

"Call me whenever it is," said Polly. "There's a phone beside my bed. And be careful. And thanks for the lunch."

"Thanks for going," Tom said. "But it was a sleeveless errand."

"It had one sleeve. We found out something. And Helen adored you."

He cupped her chin in his hand and kissed her mouth. "Tell me the rest," he said.

"What's the rest?"

"You said Helen adored—"

"And so do I," said Polly.

"That's better," Tom said. "Much better."

3

Leaving the motorcycle on the gravel of the shoulder of the road, he climbed the steps of Monty's house and knocked. All the lights were on, and the huge woman who opened the door stepped politely aside to let him squeeze past her in the narrow front hall and to reveal the half-dozen other women, along with one or two men, who were seated in the living room talking as steadily and companionably as at a church social. Through the portico to the dining-room, he could see Margy Hupp in the act of cutting a freshly frosted white cake. She was wearing the dress with the maple-leaf print and when she saw him she put the knife down, wiped her hands on a tiny apron, and held them both in his direction.

"I just heard about it, Margy," Tom said, "and I came out to tell you how sorry I am."

"You and me both," she said. Behind her clean glasses her eyes were dry. She leaned forward and kissed his cheek, a quick brush of dry lips. "You was a dear to come. Let me give you a piece of this cake. Seems like the neighbors been baking and cooking all day. Look at that." She led him to the table where covered dishes were nestled in aluminum foil and pans of rolls and a pumpkin pie were ranged as if for a food sale. "And me trying to reduce." She smoothed down the small apron. "Here, you'll want a fork, Tom. And how about some coffee?"

He ate the cake and sipped the coffee while the talk flowed on in the living room. Most of the people had dressed up for the occasion, and it was like a wake without the whiskey, though one of the men on the living-room couch, where Marge had so recently rubbed Monty's back, was nursing a can of beer. He lowered it carefully to the floor when Marge passed the cake and refilled the coffee-cups. Afterwards she pulled out a dining-room chair and sat down beside Tom.

"I got to pack sometime tonight," she said. "Got to fly to Bangor tomorrow, drive a long ways home. Funeral's the day after. Burial in the family plot at Eastport."

"Where is that, Marge?"

"Way down east. Practically up to the Canadian border. Don't tell me you ain't been to Maine." •

"No farther north than Portland."

"You'll have to come up there and pay me a call after things get settled. I ain't thought yet what I'll do. I wisht it was me and not Monty going up there in a box."

Two enormous tears formed in the corners of her eyes behind the glasses and fell unheeded onto the front of her dress. She waved away the handkerchief that Tom held out.

"You keep that. I got a whole box of Kleenex. Seems like the waterworks is working overtime."

"I don't wonder. Monty was a good man."

"They don't make them no finer," she agreed, drying her eyes vigorously. "How about a sliver of cake and a little coffee?"

Tom declined and stood up. "You've got to pack and I've got to go," he said, "unless there's something you want me to do."

She patted his shoulder. "You done the best thing you could do coming out here to see me. Monty would be pleased as punch to see you setting here. I s'pose you're going acrost to see Milliken."

"If he's still around."

"Been around all day," Marge said, "working like a beaver in freshet time. I think you'll find him over to the Coast Guard Station."

The crowd in the wardroom at the station was of another kind entirely, an assortment of men in parts of uniforms, with faces deeply tanned or burned red, all sitting in chairs ranged around the walls, a few drinking coffee or beer and most of them talking loudly in the smoky room. As Tom entered, Milliken came forward at once and guided him through the varnished door at the far end into what had once been Monty's office.

"Glad you're here," he said gruffly. "Royce said you were on the way. There's been hell to pay all day and we don't know a damn thing new except that Whitehead just died without ever regaining consciousness so we've lost whatever he might have told us." After this burst of talk, he exhaled loudly and sat down before Monty's desk.

"Royce said Monty was dead when found."

"Whole front of his chest blown out," Milliken said. "He couldn't have lived a minute. And this Whitehead, nice young fellow, lost so much blood the whole deck was awash. I don't know how he lasted as long as he did."

"Royce said their boat was aground on that island opposite Gay Head."

"That's right. Currents must have pulled them inshore and there was a breeze pushing. But we don't know where the shooting was. I had a crew tramping all over No Man's Land this morning but the report was negative. Nothing to be seen along the shore or up along the ridge, either. We rounded up all the fishermen we could find and they were negative, too. No, Tom, it must have happened on the water. A tommygun throws the casings and if they shot from the shore in the dark, they could have missed some. Couldn't have picked them all up. I had the boys crooked over looking, but all they came up with was a few shotgun shells from last fall."

"Is it known when it happened?"

"The doctor that looked at Monty thought around midnight. Of course that's a guess. It could have been eleven or one just as easily."

"No one saw any lights from the shore? What about Cora?"

"I haven't had time to call on Cora. We've been working out of here all day. Police and Coast Guard."

"I'll speak to Cora. I'm going out there from here. You know she told about seeing a car that flashed its lights out to sea."

"I *didn't* know," said Milliken, sitting up in his chair. "When was that?"

"Last time I was out there."

"But you didn't see it yourself?"

"No. She told me about it."

"You didn't mention it."

"I forgot it," Tom said. "Cora thought maybe it was kids having fun. But now it looks as if there might be something to it. It looks as if the gang is renewing operations out around Gay Head."

"I don't connect the murders," Milliken said. "The Starr kid was killed on shore and dumped over the cliff. That we know. This one last night was a seagoing operation, and it could have happened miles from here, miles from Gay Head."

"How long since you've had a murder on the Vineyard?"

Milliken pursed his lips in thought and gazed at the floor. "Four years," he said slowly. "Maybe five. Last one I recall was a knife fight between a Portuguese and a Negro in a bar. Before that it was a summer tourist that choked his wife to death. Three or four years."

"But this is three murders in one month. Really inside of two weeks. Your crime rate's going up."

"You can say that again," said Milliken. "And we don't get the first one solved before we have two more. But going back to that business about the car-lights. When did Cora say it happened?"

It was Tom's turn to gaze at the floor. "Sometime last week. I'll see if we can pin it down to a specific date. I spent a couple of days out there last week, and it was obviously before that."

"Were you planning to go out to Cora's anyway?"

"My first friend on the Vineyard," said Tom, grinning. "Yes. I want to make sure she's all right, and then I was planning to bunk at your place as before, if that's all right."

"The bed's yours," Milliken said tiredly. "If you get home before I do, leave me a note about what Cora said."

"All right. And one more thing. Could I use this phone to call Polly Harmon?"

"Be my guest," said Milliken. "Courtesy U.S. Coast Guard. And give the young lady my regards."

4

When the phone rang distantly and continuously he scrambled up the walls of sleep into the feeling that he had known all this before. Except that the last time it had been a sunny morning and now, glancing out, he saw that it was raining through scattered shreds of fog. He groped his way downstairs and silenced the noise by lifting the receiver.

"So I got you up," said Milliken's voice, jovially. "About time, too."

"What time is it?"

"Close to noon. How about some lunch at the Seagull?"

"I'll be there. Give me fifteen minutes."

"Take eighteen," Milliken said. "Then it will be noon."

"Sorry I slept so long. I didn't hear you coming or going. Did you get my note?"

"Yes. I want to talk about that and hear about Cambridge."

"About Cambridge there's something but not much. Monty's getting killed drove it all out of my head last night."

"Mine, too," Milliken said. "See you at noon."

Shaved and washed and wearing a slicker of Milliken's, he pushed open the sliding door of the diner. Ma Pierce stood behind the cash register, thin arms akimbo, old eyes alert as running mice. "That big son-of-a-bitch is down there in the booth," she shouted. "He's expecting you. Ain't you pretty with your hair all combed?"

Tom grinned at her going past and slid into the booth facing Milliken.

"So Cora thinks the business of the car lights took place on the night of the sixth and seventh or the seventh and eighth."

"She thinks it was both nights. We kept going over it and that was as close as we could get. It could have been a signal or it could have been nothing but a kid's prank."

"We may never find out," said Milliken morosely. "How were things in Cambridge?"

Tom told him in detail about the implicit connection between Dr. Summers and Freddy Starr. Milliken listened intently and asked a lot of questions, his burly shoulders hunched in the small booth.

"So there's still some room for doubt," Tom concluded.

"There usually is," Milliken said. "But what you found out makes it clear that we'd better go pay a little call on Summers. If he admits the connection, we probe some more. If he denies it, then watch him to see if he looks like a man with something to hide. Do you know him?"

"I met him once for about two minutes. He was getting off the boat when Royce brought the bike back from Woods Hole."

"So you're not exactly old friends. Would your being with me make him suspicious?"

"That depends," Tom said. "He knows I know Polly. That might help a little."

"We could take her with us when we go," Milliken said.

"I'd rather keep her out of it if there's any chance—"

"Of danger, you mean. I'd doubt there'd be danger. But let's try just you and me and see how it goes. I've got some things to clear up at the office and then we'll go over. All right with you?"

"All right," said Tom.

It was past four when they reached the outskirts of Edgartown. "Where's the house?" asked Milliken, "or do I know?"

"Water Street."

"I'd better park downtown and we'll walk. No use arousing suspicion or alerting the neighbors with a squad car before we even ring his doorbell."

"Is that why you're out of uniform?"

Milliken nodded and got out. "You're the guide," he said, moving off with his rolling gait. "It'll be dark soon, the way these clouds have closed in. What a Christ-awful day."

The rain had stopped, but the air was heavy with moisture. Sodden leaves choked the gutters and the trees, denuded now, lifted wet black boughs towards a lowering sky.

As they turned into the brick walk to the Summers place, Tom glanced across at Polly's. Her car was in the driveway but no lights were visible inside the house.

The giant knocker on the Summers front door echoed metallically in the descending gloom. There was no response, either then or after they had waited and knocked again. Tom went down the steps and around the side of the house. A light was burning in the study.

"Probably automatic," said Milliken. "Timed to snap on at dusk." He tried the knocker once more. "That noise ought to wake the dead. Do you know how the house is arranged inside?"

"Downstairs, yes. Front hall, study, corridor behind. Then another corridor and the back door into the patio. Then the boathouse."

"Is there a garage?"

"Around to the right."

"Let's prowl the premises, see if the car is there."

But the overhead door of the garage was closed and

locked and there were no windows. "No tiretracks, either," Milliken said. "What's that wall with the bobwire on top?"

"That encloses the patio or the compound, whatever you call it."

"Call it a patio," said Milliken, chuckling. "The only compound I know belongs to a good-sized family over near Hyannis. Let's go look at the boathouse. Can we get back there through Polly's yard?"

"We can try, but we'd better try now. It's getting darker by the minute."

"Are your feet as wet as mine?" asked Milliken in disgust. "Since I was a kid I've hated wet feet."

They jumped a low stone fence behind the barn and came out on a patch of sea-grass. A ten-foot canal faced with cement led in from the tidal channel to the double-doors of the boathouse.

"Closed up tight," said Milliken. "What's inside, do you know?"

"Polly says he keeps a sailboat and a power-boat."

"Can't be used except at high-tide or maybe half-tide. That could limit his sea-going. I'm not going down there to peer up under those doors. My feet are wet enough. Let's say both boats are there, but their owner is not. And let's get back to dry land."

They turned together to find themselves in the eye of a small searchlight. Polly was standing on the low stone wall.

"Ahoy, there," she called. "What's up?"

Milliken touched the brim of his hat. "Trying to find Dr. Summers. Have you seen him?"

"Not all day," said Polly. "They may have been here in the morning but I slept late. The light's on in the study, but I don't think they're there."

Milliken turned to Tom. "I'll have to get on home, but

I'd like to know when Summers comes back. Any chance of your keeping an eye on the place?"

"All right."

"He can watch from my house," said Polly cheerfully.

Tom nodded. "There's a window in her kitchen that looks across to the Summers place."

"Good," said Milliken. "Just give me a call if anything happens."

Chapter Six

1

IN THE hall of her house, the front door tightly closed and locked behind them, he began to kiss her hair, both her cheeks, the side of her neck, and then her upturned mouth.

"You're here," she said breathlessly as soon as he released her. "Legitimately, too. Doesn't that sound old-fashioned? Authorized by the police. Doesn't that sound official? Are you hungry? Would you like a drink?"

"I'm supposed to be watching, but I can do both."

Polly took his hand. "We'll hear them if they come back. Come on into the formerly medieval kitchen. We can eat, drink, and be merry, but not in that order. Doesn't that sound medieval?"

Twice in the next hour Tom went out onto the porch to scan the windows of the house next door with Polly's binoculars. The light still burned wanly in the study, but the other windows were blank and dark. When he came in the second time, she was waiting at the bottom of the staircase.

"Here," she said. "I brought you something for your expert opinion."

It was a sheet of typewriter paper folded once across.

"Good," he said. "A love letter."

"Wrong this time. It's something I found months ago. I'd

forgotten about it and then today I found it in a drawer. Look at it and tell me what you think it could be."

He unfolded the sheet and held it under the lamp. Typed on one side were three rows of capital letters:

TFZTX/NJXVB/FYGWW/UHSER/AVR/192001
ALTWM/KVWZM/CLTWN/CZYRK/VWPWF/
  GTWIE/QANHE/WPRGG/200417
UBSOL/EIXRF/VWVNF/GMTFB/FDITK/
  RWSAQ/JBXEN/MLSH/101018

She was standing close behind him, reading over his shoulder. "It looks like real gibberish," she said. "But I'd like to know what you think."

"Might be a cryptogram," said Tom. "Looks like one. Where'd you get it?"

"I got it from a book," said Polly. "There were three sheets of yellow paper folded and laid inside. Each of the sheets had just one of those lines typed on it. I typed them off with my own typewriter and put the originals back inside the book and returned the book."

"Do you remember what book it was?" asked Tom.

"I don't think it matters," she said slowly, "but I know what book it was because I was going to read it and never did. It was De Quincey's *Opium Eater*. The yellow sheets— they were carbon copies—were laid inside, folded. Or did I say that?"

"You said it, Polly. What you didn't say was where you got the book."

She cleared her throat. "It was in Dr. Summers's library."

"Where you played the piano, right?"

"That's right. But the time when I found those yellow sheets was long before that."

"How long?"

"You sound like a detective, Tom," she said, with a faint smile. "I can't remember things like that. Maybe a couple of months."

"So he lets you borrow his books?"

"That was my idea," said Polly flatly. "I was just browsing and saw the title. He didn't know I borrowed it and still doesn't. Anyway I didn't have it for long. After I found those papers in it, I got a little scared and took it back right away. Do you really think it's a cryptogram?"

"It's possible, even likely. It has the usual swatches of five letters each that make counting easier. And those numbers at the end could be some kind of signature. Maybe the initials of the sender."

"Then why are there three sets of numbers instead of their all being the same?"

"It could be that they were signed by different people. Or it could be that each message was written from a different key."

"Like music," said Polly. "But not really, I guess. Could you translate them?"

"I don't know," said Tom. "You never know with these things. Some of them go along pretty well and some take a month of Sundays. It's worth trying. But I never tried with a beautiful girl as close as you are."

"I'll go away," said Polly distantly.

"Don't go too far," said Tom, grinning. "I may need you to bathe my aching head with icepacks. Have you got a number two pencil and some scratch paper? Any paper. Graph paper would be ideal."

"I've got a legal pad upstairs," said Polly quickly. "Wait a minute."

While she was gone he scanned the lines of typing. The

simplest form of the Caesarean cipher was no good, but he would have to try the other variations. He took the pad she brought, turned it sideways, drew lines across it lengthwise, and quickly set down rows of letters. Then for almost half an hour while she sat reading on the couch, he worked at the table under the lamp, printing rapidly, counting spaces in a low voice, cursing sometimes when he made a mistake, crossing out, erasing, beginning again. At last he looked up. "The Caesarean doesn't work at all in any form," he said.

"I thought that was a baby-bearing operation."

"That's a Caesarean section. This is a cipher system that Caesar used to send military messages, and probably political instructions, back home from Gaul."

She came to sit on the arm of his chair. "How's your fevered brow?" she asked, caressing it with cool fingers. "Can you show a dumb bunny how it works?"

"It's the simplest of the systems," said Tom. "All you do is take each letter of the original message and replace it with a letter farther along in the alphabet. Always the same number of spaces—two or four or six letters along. They're called jumps."

"Suppose your letter was X and you were doing a six-jump scheme," said Polly, "what would you do, then? You'd run out of alphabet."

"Just use up what's left and start back again. On a six-jumper, X would equal D. Look, Polly." He printed eight letters in the margin of the pad: K/NQXG/AQW. "Know what that means?"

"Nope, sorry."

"That's I LOVE YOU in two-jump Caesarean."

She laughed her hearty woman's laugh. "You sound like the beginning of a rhyme by Ogden Nash:

I love you in two-jump Caesarean

Which is doubly as sweet as Bavarian."

"Good rhyme," said Tom, smiling vaguely. His mind, she saw, was obviously somewhere else. "When you take all those cryptograms together," he said, "the frequency tables don't work, either. And that's probably significant."

She was frowning. "Don't pitch them so fast, Tom. What's a frequency table?"

He cleared his throat. "In cryptanalysis the frequency tables can be important. We had them for English, French, Spanish, and German. Also Russian and Japanese and Chinese, though I stayed with the Western European languages. Except Basque. At first I could hardly believe it, but they told us that there were actually people in those countries who counted the number of times each letter of the alphabet appears in normal prose in each of those languages."

"It would drive me nutty," said Polly.

"They were probably all nuts, or else starving," said Tom. "They also counted pairs of letters, groups of three, various syllables, and even whole words. These days they do it with a computer. But if you have a photographic memory, you can make your own print-out and reconstruct the frequency tables. With a few slips, of course."

"Do you have a photographic memory?"

"No. Just pretty fair. Most of us learned the letter frequencies to save time with practice problems."

"Poe's *Gold Bug*," said Polly. "Wasn't it one of the big points that the letter E was the most common in English?"

"That's right. I don't know if Poe knew it, but it's also the most common letter in French, Spanish, and German. The order of frequency for the first nine letters in English is ETAONRISH. Nice word. Easy to remember. In French, it's even easier. The first five letters in French are EASIT."

"But none of that helps?"

"Doesn't seem to. Whoever made these lines didn't use any simple form of substitution. I have a hunch that each of these lines is attached to a different key. One thing that makes me think so is those numbers at the end."

"You called them signatures."

"Maybe so, maybe not," Tom said. "They might just as well be numerical clues that would tell the translator what key to use."

Polly sat down on the rug before the fire and pushed back her hair with both hands. "Thomas," she said, "I'm lost."

"Me, too," he said laughing. "We're lost together. But you know how when you're lost in the woods, you follow a stream if you can find one. Because that stream goes somewhere—to a river, say, and a river eventually leads you back to civilization."

She lay back with her hands behind her head. "All right, Tom, lead me back to civilization."

"I was just thinking of De Quincey's *Opium Eater.* What was the old boy's first name?"

"Same as yours," said Polly. "Thomas."

He leaned over the pad he had been using and scribbled quickly. "Wait a minute," he said. "Look at that second signature: 200417." He came and sat down beside her, brandishing the pad. "Look," he said again. "The twentieth letter is T and the fourth is D and the seventeenth is Q. How do you like that? TDQ. De Quincey's initials."

Polly sat up straight. "Q.E.D.," she said, her eyes glowing. "Tom, you're wonderful."

"Just very damn lucky," he said, his own eyes shining in the firelight. "It could be coincidence, but I don't think so.

You found these cryptograms in a book and the book was his and at the end of one of those messages are his initials in numerical notation."

"The mean thing to ask is what of it?" said Polly, smiling at his exuberance.

"I'll tell you what of it. Books. They're often used as the basis for cipher systems. I remember the Colonel telling us one day about the cleverest of the German spies, Kurt Ehrendt. For most of one year he used ciphers based on a string of novels by Dumas. The year was 1942 and the texts he used were always at the top of page forty-two of the books. In French, of course."

"So now where are we?"

"Still in the dark, but there's a little light to see by. Now what I have to do is try those other two sets of numbers—101018 and 192001."

"Do it," Polly said, "and I'll make us some coffee."

He sat down again at the table. When she came back he was gazing silently into the fire.

"Cream and sugar?"

"Just black, Polly, please."

"Are you going to tell me what you found?"

"A puzzle," he said. "Those numbers translate to JJR and STA. All I can think of is John Junior and Stanislaus. What associations do you have with JJR?"

"Here," she said. "Drink your coffee. JJR. I used to know a boy named JoJo Runyeon, but I don't think he counts. JJR. Joli Jean. He was in my elementary French reader."

"It's got to have a literary connection," said Tom, laughing. "But maybe a little higher than that."

"I'll get my dictionary," said Polly. "It has one of those lists of famous names in the back." She brought the book and laid it open under the lamplight. "Lots of R-guys," she said. "Rabelais, Rembrandt, Renoir, Robespierre. But no JJRs. Roosevelt, Rossetti."

Tom was reading ahead of her finger as it moved down the page. "Hey," he cried suddenly. "Rousseau! Jean-Jacques Rousseau! Polly, you're a genius."

"I am, aren't I?" she said smiling. "But not at making coffee. You haven't touched yours."

"It's delicious," said Tom. "You, too. But now, Polly, listen. Answer me a question."

"Listening."

"What did Rousseau write that De Quincey also wrote?"

"Books," said Polly. "Prose."

"Yes, but what kind of books?"

"Classics," she said. "Classics that obey the law of classics."

"What law is that?"

"Being dull. Did you ever try *La Nouvelle Héloise*? I did."

"You're on the wrong tack. Come back to my question."

"What was the question?"

"About Rousseau and De Quincey. They both wrote books with the same word in the title. What—"

"Confessions," said Polly contritely. "I'm sorry, Tom. I was thinking about dear Héloise and I clean forgot the confessions. So what do you think?"

"I don't know what to think. Only, couldn't it be that instead of using the novels of Dumas, the way Kurt Ehrendt did, this operative might be using books of confessions as the key to his cryptograms? That time you played the piano I saw some books of confessions in Summers's library. Remember?"

"No, I don't. I was thinking about what to play. So now where are you?"

"Coming along, but not there. The one that really bothers me is Mr. Sta. Who the hell is Mr. Sta?"

2

"You've done enough," Polly said. "Come sit by the fire. Your coffee's cold. Would you like a drink?"

"Not now, not yet," said Tom abstractedly. "I have to ride this one through. Like the good Lieutenant Milliken."

"What about Milliken?"

"Says he's a great adrenalin manufacturer. It keeps him concentrating."

"You, too?"

He watched a burned out log disintegrate and fall in rosy coals. "Maybe in a different way. Also, it's fun, like chess or anagrams."

"Letitia loves anagrams," said Polly. "When she's here she always wants to play. The only trouble is that she can't spell."

"Spelling," said Tom. "Thanks for reminding me. Where's that dictionary? Let's look under the Ss for Mr. Sta."

"Here," said Polly. "But wouldn't it be A and not S?"

"Of course," he said. "You're a genius, Polly. Now here we go. Abelard. He wrote confessions, didn't he?"

"About sleeping with Eloise, yes," said Polly.

"But his first name was Peter, it says here. All right. Marcus V. Agrippa. Wrong initials. Horatio Alger, Hans Christian Andersen. Aristotle. Did Thomas Arnold have a first name in S, like Samson or Samuel? Probably not. Artaxerxes. Nope." He snapped the book shut. "The hell with it," he said.

"Let me look," said Polly. "You skipped W. H. Auden."

"No good. Wrong initials."

"Augustine. How about Augustine?"

"No initials at all," said Tom disgustedly.

"But he was a saint," Polly persisted. "And St. stands for saint. And STA could be St. Augustine, couldn't it?"

"Hey, wait," said Tom sitting up. "He wrote confessions, right?"

"He did."

"Who's the genius again?" asked Tom.

"Me," said Polly. She was silent beside him, gazing into the fire.

"What's wrong?"

"Nothing," she said quietly. "Except that I know what you're going to say next. You're going to say that you saw that collection of books of confessions in Dr. Summers's library. And then you're going to say that those cryptograms were hidden there. So Dr. Summers must be a spy."

"That doesn't follow. Maybe he's only eccentric, like Samuel Pepys with his special shorthand. Or maybe he doesn't even know that the cryptograms are there. I'd sure like—"

"What?"

"Polly, who had that house before he bought it?"

"I don't know. It was before I ever came here. We could ask Mr. Perkins."

"Who's he?"

"The old man you met outside the day you came to call, the one that said my name was Polly."

"All right, we'll ask him. Who else besides you has access to Summers's library?"

"Only Otto."

"Maybe they're his messages. What about a cleaning woman?"

"Otto does that, when it's done, which isn't often. The first time I was there a huge cobweb covered both pedals on the piano. But you started to say something."

"I've forgotten."

"You said you'd like to do something, but you didn't say what."

"Oh. I was going to say that I'd like to get in there and go through the books near the one where you found the cryptograms. There might be more pieces of paper with messages, or records, or whatever they are. We could see if the key numbers are the same—if they *are* key numbers. Also, I'd like to have a look at one of those books of confessions, just to see if they're going to be of any help with the cryptograms—if they *are* cryptograms."

"You couldn't do it now, Tom. Dr. Summers might have come back."

"I didn't mean right now. But that's an idea. Does this town have a public library?"

"You're thinking they might have one of those volumes of confessions?"

"What do you think?"

"They might," she said. "Back in the shadowy sections. Up front they have fiction and detective stories and the latest Book-of-the-Month selection that everyone snatches up first."

Tom stood up quickly. "Let's go look in the shadowy sections."

"We couldn't now. It's closed. They're only open three days a week in winter."

"Just when the islanders need the library most."

"They all have television."

"Who's the librarian?"

"Mr. Perkins's daughter, Susan."

"Would she be home? Could you call her? Would she let us into the library?"

"I think," said Polly, smiling at his eagerness, "that the answer to all three of your probing questions would be yes."

Outside it was full dark. A cold wind had sprung up and a few stars showed faintly. Along the walks was the smell of damp leaves. When they had borrowed the key and let themselves in, the old library building was as silent and as dank as a tomb, and at first they could not find the lights. The card file showed no entries for Augustine or Rousseau, but there was one old copy of De Quincey's *Opium Eater*. Polly signed the yellow card and they walked back through the gusty streets. The fire had burned low in the grate, and there was a pleasant feeling of home. When Polly disappeared upstairs, Tom turned on the light in the dining-room and opened the musty volume.

"I here present you, courteous reader," said De Quincey, "with the record of a remarkable period in my life; and according to my application of it, I trust that it will prove, not merely an interesting record, but, in a considerable degree, instructive."

You couldn't ask for anything better than that, Tom thought. Interest and instruction at the same time. A little pompous, of course, but you were not judging De Quincey's style. Only using his words as the possible basis of a cryptogram. He read on rapidly to the end of the section and found the notation: "Original preface, 1821." The actual beginning of the book itself went better: "I have often been asked how it was, and through what series of steps, that I became an opium eater. Was it gradually, tentatively, mistrustingly, as one goes down a shelving beach into a deepening sea?"

That image of the beach and the sea was attractive enough, he thought, especially to a cryptographer at work on Martha's Vineyard. He reached for the legal pad and the Blackwing pencil and quickly made a chart in four parallel columns which he labelled JUMP, KEY, PLAIN, and CIPHER. This was the way we used to do with the running key cryptograms, he thought. He counted the number of characters in the cipher: forty-one. "All right," he said aloud, and copied down the first forty-one characters of De Quincey's opening sentence: IHAVEOFTENBEEN-ASKEDHOWITWASANDTHROUGHWHAT. Next he assigned the jump numerals to each of De Quincey's letters. Step Three, filled with careful counting, was the deciphering step, always remembering to jump from right to left.

In fifteen minutes he saw that it would not work at all. The line in his chart labelled PLAIN offered nothing but gibberish. "All right," he said, again out loud, and turned back to the opening of De Quincey's preface, making a fresh chart and working as before.

This time it felt better. ALTWM came out to SEPFI. The second unit, KVWZM, produced VESHI, and the third became PSVIT. It looked impossible and even silly, but he still remembered the advice of Colonel Webb. "Print it out," he had said, "like a Roman inscription on a tomb. Those five-letter swatches are arbitrary. Print it out, and the words of the message will appear, if they're there."

He worked rapidly through the rest of the swatches and completed his print-out without word divisions:

SEPFIVESHIPSVITALEARRIVEOCTTEN
USUALPLACE

Then, as he entered the final letter and glanced back, his heart leaped. This made sense. It was a clear directive, dated 5 September, to the ship *San Vitale* to arrive at the usual place (wherever that might be) on 10 October.

But where? Bringing what? And to whom? There was no way of knowing unless the other cryptograms provided a clue. The big gain here was that the hunch about the confessions cipher was working, and what worked for De Quincey might work also for Augustine and Rousseau. And where were the saint and the sophist? On the bookshelves of the house next door, not fifty yards away.

Except for the fragrance he would not have known she was there until her arms came round him from behind the chair and her face came down so that her cheek rested against his own. He turned and stood, to see that she was barefoot and wearing a quilted robe of dark green. Her cheeks were rosy and when he held her lightly against him he knew that under the robe she was naked. He opened the front and bent to kiss her breasts. White as snow, warm as toast, and ornamented with strawberries. He spoke the words into her ear and began under the robe to caress the small of her back. Her eyes shining, her head thrown back, she was gazing gravely into his face while his hands moved over the smoothness of her back and the curves of her hips. When she spoke at last, it was almost matter-of-factly.

"I've never shown you where I sleep, have I? I've taken over Letitia's room and there's a big bed with a canopy."

He gathered her up, tightly now, and his voice was husky. "Let's go there," he said.

3

After the transport and the slow descent to the knowledge of where they had been and where they were now, they lay side by side, her head cradled in the crook of his arm, her dark hair spread on the pillow, and her eyes still shining in the faint nightlight which had been all they had needed.

"We're wonderful," she said. "Aren't we perfect?"

"Better than any other perfection you can name. And if you want another opinion, we've been wasting a lot of time until tonight."

"I couldn't before. At first it was too soon. Then I was shy, and after that it was just the wrong time. Now's the right time."

"So we have it," Tom said fervently. "Let's keep it, forever and a day."

Her breath was warm against his ear. "That's lover-talk, Tom. Forever is a long time, and forever and a day is a whole day longer. But talk me some more lover-talk."

"I love you, Polly," he said. "How's that for original lover-talk?"

"I hope it's not just talk."

"Hardly. Remember the electrical currents."

"My legs were like water. I didn't think they'd hold me up. Almost from the first. No, I won't lie for modesty's sake. *From* the first. Something about you turned me on."

"Galvanized is one of the terms."

"Like a drainspout? How awful. I don't feel galvanized."

"Well, you did it to me. And you drove my great achievement clean out of my head."

"What great achievement?"

"Cracking the cipher. I had just finished when you came with your lovely—"

"How funny," Polly said. "There you were downstairs trying to crack a cipher and I was upstairs trying to decide—"

"What perfume to wear."

"No, silly, whether to come down there in just the robe."

"I'm glad you decided."

"Only glad?"

"Delighted."

"Me, too," she said with great contentment. "That's what I decided, and what did you decide?"

"That I love you."

"I meant about the cipher."

"I can't decide," Tom said. "It's a very curious message, even after it's deciphered. It's a directive of some kind, dated September fifth, and ordering a ship called the *San Vitale* to arrive October tenth at the usual place."

"That's all it said?"

"All it said. It was the De Quincey cipher. Of course the message might have been for last fall or the year before."

"I don't think so," Polly said. "The papers in the book were fresh, not old. I'm thinking very clearly now, Tom, after what we just deliciously did, and I'll tell you the oddest thing about it. October tenth was the day we went to Cambridge."

"Nope," said Tom. "I'm thinking even more clearly after what we did—"

"Deliciously."

"More than deliciously. And the day we went to Cambridge was the eleventh."

Polly sat up suddenly. "Then it's even stranger, Tom. Because the night before that was the tenth and that's when Monty Hupp was shot. And look. Oh, look. Who sent us off to Cambridge?"

"Milliken."

"Could he have wanted us out of the way?"

"For what?"

"Because he knew the tenth was the day."

"It was the eleventh," said Tom patiently.

"Ships can be late," said Polly. "Storms, engine troubles, mutinies, any number of reasons."

"You can't be serious, Polly. Milliken's all wool and a yard wide. Now if it was Royce—"

"But it wasn't Royce. You said yourself it was Milliken who sent us. He telephoned that night, remember? He said he'd book us seats on the Boston plane. Why was he calling you that night of all nights?"

"He had a good reason."

"What?"

"He wanted to solve the Freddy Starr murder."

"So we went and saw Helen and checked in Widener and came back and Monty Hupp was dead."

"So you're saying Milliken shot him?"

"No. That's not it. I'm saying he wanted to get us out of the way because he knew there might be shooting and he didn't want you to be killed. Or me either."

"That's different. But how could Milliken know about October tenth? The only people that knew about it were the conspirators, and we only know about it now because we cracked their cipher."

"You, not we. *You* cracked their cipher."

"A little too late. If I'd had it earlier we might have saved Monty. There's another thing about October tenth."

"Spill it, bub," she said, nestling against him.

"All right. What happened that morning?"

"Oh, lord, Tom. I can't even remember what happened yesterday morning."

"I was out there at Cora's. Then in the afternoon you drove out to pick me up. We came here for dinner. And then what?"

"We went to the house next door and I played—"

"Because they weren't there."

"I remember. They left in the car on the *Islander* that morning."

"The morning of the tenth. So the problem is where they went. We just possibly might find out, especially if they went to Cambridge. Where else would they have gone?"

"I thought Brown and Yale, but I'm not certain," said Polly.

"Milliken could get help on that from the police in Providence and New Haven. Or maybe more likely the State Police in Rhode Island or Connecticut."

"How?"

"Provide a description and a date. Have them check it out at the university libraries, see if anyone remembers a visit from the distinguished Dr. Summers and his tall henchman. I'll bet that the answer would be no. At Yale and Brown, I mean."

"What makes you think so?"

"Because Cambridge is easier to get to. Because Summers is well known there, at least around the Yard and the libraries. Because he could have shown up there to establish an alibi, just in case he should need one, and then left with Otto for the ship *San Vitale* to get whatever it was that they got. And Milliken could help there, too. If the *San Vitale* put in at Boston Harbor, or any of the other harbors where records are kept, the facts could be found out."

"But not No Man's land or the Elizabeth Islands."

"They don't keep records or anything else on No Man's Land," Tom said.

She was running the tip of her tongue across the top of his ear.

"That tickles," he said.

"That's why I'm doing it. You've thought of an awful lot of checking, Tom. Three universities and all those harbors. Don't you think it could wait until tomorrow?"

He did not answer. Instead his arms came round her and for a long time neither of them spoke.

4

Much later she awoke from a deep sleep, wanting to remember and, remembering, reached out to touch Tom's shoulder. But the bed-space beside her was empty. When he did not return, she snapped on the light and peered at the clock on the bedside table. The hands pointed to three-twenty. She pulled on the dark-green bathrobe and moved barefoot to the top of the stairway, calling his name. There was no answer and she ran downstairs to find him hunched over the counter in the kitchen, with two books at his elbow and before him a scattering of yellow sheets covered with his neat printing. He heard her and looked up and smiled.

"So here you are," she said. "Hard at work in the middle of the night."

"A good time," he said. "No interruptions."

"You mean until now. Would you like some coffee?"

"Had some. The cup's in the sink. Uncracked, I hope. But the ciphers are cracked."

She went across and put her hand on his shoulder. "You're some kind of genius," she said. "How did you manage that?"

"Easit," he said. "I borrowed the key and filched Rousseau and St. Augustine from Summers's library. The house was quiet and empty. And I found another cipher inside a copy of the *Confessio Amantis*. So, by hook and crook and guesswork we have three more, four in all. Look here, Polly. It's really what we've been calling it—a conspiracy."

She read the yellow sheets he slid along the counter:

1. NOV TEN SECURE SLIDES ROUEN
2. MUST HAVE NORTH AFRICAN ORIGINALS OCT FIFTEEN
3. AUG TWO BOURGES REPLICAS LEFT 0600 ADVISE WHEN SHIPPING ORIGINALS

"They're not in order," said Tom. "That third one was the one I found in the other book. Here's the first one we did. Call it Number Four." He handed her the copy:

4. SEP FIVE SHIP S VITALE ARRIVE OCT TEN USUAL PLACE

"It's still gibberish to me," said Polly.

"Well, not exactly. But a few things come clear. Take this San Vitale message. At first I read it wrong. That San Vitale isn't a ship at all. The word *ship* is a verb, not a noun. It's a directive to ship, that is, to *send* something, from or of San Vitale. And look here."

He spread a creased and crumpled sheet before her and pointed to one of the items.

"This is that book-list of borrowings that we copied out at Harvard. I've been carrying it around in my billfold. Look."

He had placed his finger beside Jusserot's *Les trésors d'art religieux du San Vitale*.

"So you think—" she began to say.

"I think," he said slowly, "that the shipment that arrived on the tenth of October at what they call the usual place was some kind of treasure. And I think the usual place was somewhere at sea off Gay Head. And I think Monty Hupp and Whitehead intercepted them and got killed."

Polly was gazing at him with wide eyes. "Treasure? What kind of treasure?"

"What it says in Jusserot's title: treasures of religious art."

"But paintings would be known. They'd be missed. They'd be recognized."

"I didn't mean paintings," said Tom. "Look at this third message: AUG TWO BOURGES REPLICAS LEFT 0600 ADVISE WHEN SHIPPING ORIGINALS."

"Originals, replicas. I don't get it."

"Take it from the top," said Tom. "Apart from crown jewels and the famous collections in the museums, the greatest single repository of treasure of all sorts is probably the Church, including the Eastern Orthodox. It's been around a long time; it owns hundreds of thousands of acres of real estate, thousands of paintings and murals both wonderful and awful, and then treasure."

"You mean coins and jewels?"

"Here I think it's jewels. Bishops' mitres encrusted with rubies, crucifixes decorated with emeralds and diamonds. Opals, sapphires. And pearls. Think of all the wealthy merchants in the old days who kept out of Hell and paved their way to the pearly gates with pearls. Or the so-called precious stones."

"Cat's eyes," said Polly. "Topaz."

"In those messages," said Tom, "you notice the words *originals* and *replicas*. Evidently somehow they've been sending replicas to replace the originals and then shipping the originals over here. For what you might call processing and resale."

"But how could they make acceptable replicas at this distance?"

"It wouldn't be easy, but it would be possible. First they'd take many pictures from all angles. That message I numbered one says: NOV TEN SECURE SLIDES ROUEN. That would be Rouen Cathedral, and the directive seems to date from last fall, a year ago. SECURE SLIDES."

"But they'd be seen taking pictures."

"There are ways to avoid being seen. Our old Colonel Webb in Germany was full of wonderful stories about Gustav Kröger, the cleverest agent in western Europe. Kröger managed to photograph hundreds of pages of top secret documents, and according to the colonel he's still at large. Or still was when I left Germany."

"How did he do it?"

"I don't know how he got into the files but I know the

kind of camera he used. It's called a Minox, with a built-in light-meter. It carries an ultrasensitive 9.5 millimeter film strip with fifty exposures, and the exposed strip is small enough to conceal in a watchband or a belt-buckle or a bridge."

"A bridge?"

"A dental bridge. One of the falsest things about Kröger was his teeth. But these people here apparently use colored slides. With those and the measurements, a really clever craftsman could make a replica of the original that no one but an expert could recognize as false. After it's ready, they substitute it for the real thing and send the original over here. Probably they pry out the valuable jewels from the crucifixes and the mitres and the picture frames and destroy what's left. But that's a guess. Most of what I just said is guessing, except about Kröger."

"Professor Harriman at Harvard used to call it an empirically probable hypothesis. But it's all incredible," said Polly.

"You'd be less likely to think so if you'd heard my old colonel's stories. The thing about this is that it's slow. But it evidently pays off or else they wouldn't be doing it."

Tom pushed back his chair and stood up, stretching his arms and yawning widely. "Those books have to go back into that library," he said, through the yawn.

"Can't it wait?"

"Better not. They might come home and notice the gaps on the shelves. They know you have the key to the house. The first thing they'd do is come searching over here."

"I could hide the books in the attic."

"They might not find them, but they'd find you. And if they operate the way I think they do, they'd find ways of making you talk. These people have a good thing going, and they're going to keep it going. They're ready to kill. They've killed."

He picked up the key from the corner of the table and leaned to peer through the window. "I'd better go now," he said. "It's still dark as pitch."

Polly stood so close to him that he felt the silkiness of the green bathrobe and the warmth beneath it. "Let me come with you," she whispered.

"No, not a chance. It won't take five minutes. I know the room and the location of the shelves. I could do it in the dark." He slid into his jacket and picked up the books. "Better put out this light and wait for me here. What time is it now?"

"Half past four," said Polly. "You said five minutes. I'll expect you at four thirty-five." She kissed him quickly at the front door, closed it behind him, and sat down in the dark by the kitchen window to wait.

The antique clock in the hall ticked loudly in the quiet of the house and she found herself counting the strokes of the pendulum. Sixty, eighty, a hundred. She wondered if every tick was actually a second and in wondering lost her count. She found that her hands were tightly clenched, and spread them flat on the table top, taking up the count once again. At three hundred she would go out and look at the clock in the dim light that trickled down from the upper hall. But it suddenly surprised her by striking a single tinny note: four-thirty. It was slow. She should have remembered that it was slow. It had always been slow, and she ought to have remembered. To hell with this black-out. She went to the wall-switch in the kitchen, and flashed the light on and off quickly. The hands of the kitchen clock showed a quarter to five.

He said five minutes and now it's fifteen, she thought. Soon it will be dawn. He's found some more of those ciphers and he's copying them down. Let him come back. Let him come now. He has enough ciphers. Perhaps it's something else. He's dropped the key and is trying to find it. Or he decided to check that basement room. He was on the stairs and the door locked behind him. He can't get out. Or he did and he's outside in the compound trying to scale that wall. I won't wait any longer. I can't. It's physically impossible.

She ran upstairs and pulled on sweater, skirt, and sneakers. Whatever it was, something was wrong. As she hurried down the stairway, the antique clock cleared its throat hoarsely and banged out its tinny anthem. Five by the slow clock. He's been gone more than half an hour and he said five minutes. Really wrong, really wrong, really wrong.

She left the front door ajar behind her as she ran down the steps and across the lawn between the two houses. She found to her amazement that her eyes were filled with tears and stopped under the aged maple to dry them on the sleeve of her sweater.

When she looked up, it was to see the house bulking whitely in the faint glow from the distant streetlamp, and something else that stopped her shivering by the black bole of the old tree.

The Mercedes was standing in the driveway.

Chapter Seven

1

WHEN HE opened his eyes there was nothing to see but the darkness. The pressure on the back of his head and his shoulders could only be a wall. His feet at the ankles and his hands at the wrists were tightly bound, and something else, a strap or a chain, constricted his chest and pinioned his upper arms. His head and the side of his jaw ached steadily. With what seemed a great effort he rolled his body until the pressure of the wall was gone and he lay on his side along the hard floor. It was then that he became conscious of the sound.

Low-pitched, shrill, raw, and intermittent, it sounded like a lathe or a dentist's drill. It had been silent for some minutes when a door scraped open and dim light filtered in from the room beyond. The place where he lay was small, a storage closet of some kind. Boxes were piled in tiers along the two walls he could see. Footsteps rasped on the cement floor and a face bent down towards his own: plump, bespectacled, pale, and bald, with a fringe of gray-white hair and many wrinkles.

"So you have come arount," the man said. "The sound of my skeep woke you up." He stooped to lift Tom's head. "That's right. Groan some more. It hurts. Of course it hurts. Take a drink." He was holding a cup against Tom's lips.

"What is it?"

"Nossing but water."

Tom drank it all and felt his head gently lowered again to the floor. "Who are you?" he asked.

"Never mind. The man from Samaria. Here, I lift the aching head once more." The cushion he slid under it smelt strongly of mildew.

"Why are you helping me?"

"For charity. You have been hurt. You are in danger. I helped many in the war. Young like you."

"Where was that?"

"Nederlands."

"My hands and feet are tied."

"You are a prisoner."

"In the basement of the house. Is that it?"

"Just so. I know you. I have seen you before."

"Upstairs in the library. You were the silent one who came along the hall and stood behind the door."

The old man nodded, his spectacles glinting in the dim light. "The young lady was playing. I saw you and came back to the shop."

"Shop? What shop?"

The old man waved a heavily veined hand over his shoulder. "Out there. Where I live and work."

"What do you do?"

"Lapidarius," he said. "I am by profession a lapidary."

"What is that?"

"A carver of stones, precious stones, like my father and my grandfather."

"Then carve these ropes and free my hands."

"I would not dare."

"You helped others to escape. You said so. Why not now?"

"At that time it was not like this time. Then I was in my own house in my own country. We hide British, Free French, sometimes Americans. We pass them along in our famous resistance against the Nazis."

"Nazis like Otto?"

"He is not Nazi—*was* not, I mean. I think he was Communist. A Yugoslav. Black Yugoslav. Of Croatia."

"Was he the one who slugged me?"

The old man nodded. "And dragged you here. He is strong and dangerous. Also cruel."

"Why don't you get away?"

"Do you mean escape? Leave? This we cannot do."

"We? You and I?"

"The professor and me."

"Is Summers the professor?"

"The name is not Summers. Sommerabend is his name. Sommerabend, once of Weimar." The old man smiled to himself. "Soft like an evening in summer. But he is very learned. Before the *scandale* he was making his index to Christian iconology."

"What was the scandal?"

"The scandal of Weimar. You have not heard of this? Of course, it was not heard of. It was hushed up. The ring of male prostitutes at the university. He was in disgrace and starving in Berlin when Otto found him."

"I took Otto as the chauffeur, the servant."

"A pretence," the old man said. "Here, quickly, lie down. Let me remove the pillow. Someone is coming." He hurried out and closed the door.

Flat on the cement in the dark, Tom lay and listened to the voices on the far side of the door. There were two: the old man and another. He could hear the rhythms but not the words. After a time he understood why the rhythms sounded so odd, so un-English. The language was German, or possibly Dutch. If I were there in the room with them, he thought, I could tell what they are saying, the gist of it anyway.

"So," said a voice clearly just outside the door. "I go to see our handsome young friend."

The door scraped open again raspingly and a man stood silently there. Tom could hear his breathing for a long minute before he spoke.

"He says that you are awake."

Tom did not answer.

Heels clicked across the floor in three strides. The thin, ascetic face of Dr. Summers, vulpine, beak-nosed, and topped with the shock of iron-gray hair, loomed into view in the dim light from the room beyond. Tom saw that he was wearing a hound's-tooth jacket and a paisley scarf.

"So, your eyes are open," Summers said.

"In more ways than one," said Tom.

"Can you see in the dark? What were you doing in my study without a light?"

"Returning books."

"Is this true? What books were these and how did you get them?"

"They were two books of confessions. The confessions of St. Augustine and the confessions of Jean-Jacques Rousseau."

"You are interested in confessions?"

"I'm making a study of them," said Tom.

"You have not replied to my other question: how did you get the books?"

"I borrowed the key to the house and went in and borrowed the books. I was bringing them back when your man Otto slugged me."

"You borrowed the key? From whom?"

"From the girl next door. It was the middle of the night and she did not know I was taking it," said Tom, and thought: Up to now I have not lied to this man; but why shouldn't I lie? Summers himself would not hesitate to lie. His whole life is a lie. All right, then, tell him a lie. "It was still in my pocket," he said aloud, "from the time when she brought me here to listen to her playing of the piano upstairs."

"This is my fault," said Summers. "A stupid oversight because I trusted my young friend. I should have taken back the key. My house is filled with priceless possessions."

"Your friend would not have taken anything," Tom said. "She has many valuable possessions of her own, and she has no use for yours."

"So? I would not have believed this. But you say it. Tell me, what possessions?"

"Youth," said Tom. "And beauty. And honesty, and perfect white teeth."

"You are being ironic at an old man's expense."

"You asked me to name her possessions. I named them. There are others that I have not named."

"Never mind. I see your point. Spare me your ironies. You are young and witty. Too witty, perhaps."

"Is that possible?"

"To be too witty? Certainly," Summers said. "Look. You are lying on your back in a basement room. There is blood in the corner of your mouth and your jaw is swollen. Your hands and feet are tied with rope and there is a leather strap around your shoulders. All that is now necessary, with these magnificent preparations, is to add one heavy anchor around your neck and to drop you over the side. Then you, and your wit, and your ironies all vanish together in the bottom of the sea."

His voice had risen as he spoke, but Tom ignored the tone. "Over the side of what?" he asked scornfully.

"Over the side of my speedboat. Another of my valuable possessions."

"If you could get it out. But you can't get it out. It's low tide."

"How do you know this?"

"I checked before I came," lied Tom. "The tide was going out."

"But you do not know what time it is now."

"My watch tells me," said Tom. "Your man didn't steal my watch. It is half past two in the afternoon."

"No," said the other smoothly. "You have lost a day. It is half past six in the evening. The tide is high. We will take a little pleasure-trip on my boat."

Tom felt his courage ebbing. Could this be so? Had he, in fact, been knocked out for most of the day? It was impossible. Summers was lying.

"That's a lie," he said, with more confidence than he felt. "It's morning and the tide is out. Your boat is immovable."

"That is easily found out," Summers said. He moved to the door and spoke in German to the old man. But the words had nothing to do with boats or tides. All he wanted was a chair. The old man brought one in—a sturdy kitchen chair—and placed it near Tom's feet. Summers sat down, crossed his legs, and leaned forward.

"Tell me. How much do you know?"

"About what subject?"

"Let us say about my life."

Through the pain in his swollen jaw, Tom grinned in the

half-light. So he's trying another tack, he thought. "The girl next door—" he began.

"We know her name," said Summers. "Polly. Polly Harmon."

"She says that you are a wonderful man. You are a scholar. You study at Harvard, sometimes at Yale. Your hobbies are sailing and gardening and reading. You have many books. You are wealthy. You keep a Mercedes and a chauffeur named Otto."

"All this is correct," said Summers. "Please continue."

"You make frequent trips to the mainland," said Tom. "The purpose is pleasure and to examine the art collections at the universities. Your interest is in Christian iconology. In this field you are very learned. You also employ the aged artisan out there. He cares for your valuable possessions and repairs them when they are broken. It is a rich life and a full one."

Summers smiled. "So it is," he said. "Therefore you can scarcely blame me for wishing to keep it so."

"Cut off these ropes and chain up your dog and let me out of here and you can have it," said Tom quickly.

"My dog?"

"Your mastiff, Otto."

"I see," said Summers, faintly smiling. "And you would not prefer charges?"

"Against Otto perhaps."

"He was only doing his duty. A watchdog, as you said. You yourself were the intruder."

"Then the charges would be easily dismissed."

"Tell me, Mr. —"

"Cook."

"Yes, Cook. I remember the introduction at the boat. Tell me, have you told me all you know?"

"What else is there?"

"I am asking you."

"I've told you," said Tom defiantly.

The chair scraped harshly on the cement as Summers pushed it back and stood up. "Mr. Cook, I wish I could believe you, but I think you are keeping something back. We will have to discover what it is. Perhaps by the use of the watchdog. What did you call him? The mastiff. That will please him."

2

Behind Summers's retreating footsteps the hall door slammed in the house above. At once the little lapidary reappeared in the store-room and took his station at Tom's feet.

"I could not help hearing what he said."

"Neither could I," said Tom, sardonically.

"You were perhaps a little too defiant."

"Whistling in the dark," said Tom. "Tell me, was I right in guessing that it is still early morning?"

The little man nodded. "Soon it will be dawn."

"Is the tide high or low?"

"I am sorry. I do not know about the tides."

"What was that word you used before? For your machine?"

The old man shook his head. "Machine? My skeep, do you mean?"

"What is that?"

"It is a kind of wheel for polishing. It is made of iron and it whirls fast or slowly. I mix olive oil with the dust of diamonds. This is the polishing agent for the precious stones. Here today it is a ruby, very large. This is from Bourges, the prize of their collection. Formerly in the crown of a prince of the Church. Excuse me, someone is coming."

He ran out into the workroom, leaving the door open. Footfalls echoed heavily on the stairs. The huge form of Otto bulked in the small doorway. He was wearing boots, to which specks of sand adhered.

"So we go," he said. His voice was deep, and he gave a V sound to the W. He bent down and lifted Tom as easily as if he had been a child or a light duffel-bag. He was wearing a thick navy shirt that smelt of rancid sweat. With Tom over his shoulder, he took the stairs two at a time, and dumped him face up on the rug beside the piano. He was breathing heavily and he stood for a moment grinning down.

"How you feel, Mr. Cook? Not so good. Your jaw is swollen. Somebody must have hit you." His large hands tested the knots in the ropes that bound Tom's hands and feet. "All tight. Good job. You like to take a little ride?"

Summers had come to stand beside him. "I advise you against it," he said. "The house may be watched."

"Who would watch it?" said Otto scornfully. "A sea gull on the roof?"

"The girl must know he came here, and that he has not returned. She could be watching."

"The girl is young. She would be sleeping. It is still dark. The young girls sleep in the dark." He laughed suddenly, as at some private joke. But he crossed the room to peer between the draperies to the house next door. "All dark there," he said, coming back. "We leave in the dark. One minute and we are away. Give me the tape."

"There is no need for tape," Summers said.

"Give me the tape," said Otto, again. He held out his hand.

"I have no tape. I am against the use of tape."

A sound like a curse rumbled deep in Otto's throat and he raised a heavy fist in a threatening gesture. When Summers ignored it, Otto turned and left the room. Soon he was back, kneeling beside Tom's head, peeling the tape from the roll. "Lift up his head," he said gruffly to Summers, but the other only turned his back.

Rolling Tom on his side, Otto stretched the tape across his mouth and around the back of his head to the front. Then he tore off another long strip and began to apply a second layer.

"Keep the nostrils clear," said Summers. "I am warning you. He must breathe through the nostrils."

"Thank you, Herr Professor Doktor," said Otto. "You are a very clever man. Now we go. Where is Junius?"

"In his shop."

"Tell him to stay there," said Otto. "He can work if he wishes, but he must stay there."

"Tell him yourself," said Summers. "He's yours, not mine."

"Never mind," said Otto. "He will stay." He lifted Tom to his shoulder and strode to the back hall. "Come along," he said brusquely. In the dark of the corridor he stumbled on the steps, recovered his balance, and swung open a door.

All garages smell alike, thought Tom. So it will be a car-ride, not a boat-ride. There was a jingle of keys.

"Put him in the back," came Summers's voice. "Cover him with a blanket."

"I have no blanket and it is late. He goes in the trunk. Here, bend your legs," he said to Tom. "You are a tall boy, a strong and beautiful boy, but you will fit."

The lid came down and latched over Tom, who lay hunched in the gasoline-smelling darkness. Like an unborn child, he thought. He heard the engine whir and catch and above it the rumble of the opening door. The car backed out and the door rumbled shut. They were moving now. He could hear nothing but the sound of the motor.

Keep count of the turns, he told himself. And the time between the turns. He stretched out his feet as far as he could, trying vainly for comfort in the narrow trunk.

At what must have been the end of the driveway the car turned left and accelerated. So they are going through the town, he thought. They are taking the chance of being seen in the town. He heard the tires squeal as the car took the right-hand turn. Now they were going fast. A left, then a right. It could only be the road to West Tisbury. How far was it? Ten miles? If they stayed on that road there would be a little time to think.

He lay in the dark and thought of Polly. When he did not return, she would have waited. How long? Fifteen minutes? At the most, half an hour. He saw her in the dark jacket and blue jeans and sneakers crossing the lawn under the old trees, keeping to the shadows the streetlight threw, climbing the granite steps and trying the front door. Under the tape his mouth went dry and he thought of the front door wrenched open, the girl seized, the strong arm around her throat.

But it had not happened. Unless they had been pretending for his benefit there in the library-study, Polly was still at large. Wherever she was, she was safe from them, at least for the time being.

He tried to remember her as she had looked in the dark-green robe, gazing up into his face, her gray eyes fixed on his. But the car braked so suddenly that he had to flex his muscles to avoid rolling forward. He had lost count of the time. How much had it been? Ten minutes? Certainly no more than twenty.

Otto, the pseudo-chauffeur, would be driving. Why had he slowed down? Perhaps for the road to the airport. But the car had not turned there. It was picking up speed again. He lay back, all his muscles aching, trying to pay attention and to think at the same time.

What would Polly have done? Scaled the wall into the compound, gone to see if the speedboat was still in the boat-house? No. She would have done the sensible thing, which meant calling the substation at Oak Bluffs, reporting to Mil-liken, asking his help. Suppose Milliken was at home asleep. Royce or the other man would have taken the call and told Polly where Milliken was.

The Mercedes was slowing down once more. The motor purred and chuckled and the car climbed briefly, levelled off, and repeated the process. Then it stopped and he heard both front doors slam in succession. A key explored the lock, the lid of the trunk opened like a mouth, and air poured in that smelt of hay. There was light to see by now, the sun had risen, and Otto's face under the visor of the long-billed cap was peering in at Tom.

"You are still alive," he said. Suddenly he frowned. "Too bad. We do not have to dig your grave yet." He lifted Tom from the trunk and lowered him to the floor. From one of his pockets he produced the roll of tape. "Only now we tape the eyes," he said.

Summers moved quickly, striking the tape from his hand in one sudden downward thrust. "No tape on the eyes," he yelled angrily. "You are a beast. Take the tape from his mouth now. There is no one to hear him. And no tape on the eyes."

Otto shouldered him aside and bent to retrieve the tape. Summers kicked him hard in the ribs and Otto, springing up, struck him backhanded across the mouth. The force of the blow knocked Summers off his feet and for a long minute he lay back as if stunned, with Otto bending fiercely over him.

"Take the tape from his mouth," mimicked Otto, mockingly, in falsetto. "No tape on the eyes. Do you give me orders? Remember dear Friedrich. Your little boy-friend Friedrich with the soft round face and the curls?" Otto was shouting now, his voice rising with his anger. "Remember his little round ass, professor? Remember how he looked with his head in his lap? Not your lap, Professor. *His?*"

3

In the heavy silence that followed, Tom gazed around the cavernous room. Chinks of morning light showed through the worn shingles of the roof and the warped boards of the siding. Above his head was a disused haymow, and beyond the wide door stretched a winding lane, bordered with jackpines. Somewhere out of sight a song-sparrow sang four bright notes, chirred, and stopped.

Summers was standing now, dabbing at his mouth with the paisley scarf from his neck. After his outburst, Otto had disappeared, his boots echoing across the hollow planks.

"I do not find the tarp," he said, coming back.

"In the back of the pick-up."

"It is not there," growled Otto.

"You were the last to use it," said Summers with immense scorn, "for your filthy operation."

Otto kicked savagely at one of the rear tires of the car. "I told you to put it back," he roared.

"And I told you," said the lighter voice of Summers, "that I would never touch it again."

They sounded, thought Tom, like a married couple snarling at each other over a misplaced blanket from their bed. Was this, after all, a clue to their real relationship, or was it merely a business arrangement, a marriage of convenience?

Otto cleared his throat and spat contemptuously on the floor at Summers's feet.

"It was covered with his blood," cried Summers, with a sound like a sob. "Murderer. Butcher."

"Murderer, butcher," repeated Otto mockingly. "And what do we say of you, with your Wilhelms and your Friedrichs, the gay little boys with their lipstick and their blue eyeshadow!"

"Your axes and your knives," shouted Summers, "and your greasy Communist whores in the slums of Belgrade."

"Far from Belgrade," said Otto. "Fighting in the mountains with the free men, not starving in the slums of Berlin with little gay boys for company."

He turned away once more, his bootfalls receding across the floor. From a distance Tom heard an engine catch, cough, and catch again. A gray pick-up truck backed slowly out and stopped beside the Mercedes.

"Now we go," Otto said. "Cover his eyes."

"Remove the tape," said Summers imperiously. "I have a band for his eyes."

Otto knelt down beside Tom and began peeling back the outer layer of tape. "You say nothing. Remember, no sound." With the side of his hand he made a slicing motion across Tom's throat. "You understand?"

Tom nodded and lay still.

Summers stood watching. "It is true," he told Tom. "You must not speak. He has slit many throats. He would certainly do it again."

The knife glinted in Otto's hand. He yanked the tape from Tom's mouth, sawed it in two with the blade of the knife, and jerked it away from his cheeks. "Now the band," he said. "And quickly. It is late." He seized the scarf from Summers and bound it tightly around Tom's eyes, rolling him half over to tie it behind his neck. With even less effort, seemingly, he lifted Tom's body, dropped him with a thump into the bed of the truck, and backed the vehicle slowly down the incline from the barn.

The route Otto followed could only have been a rough country lane, up hill and down dale, with many curves and bone-jarring potholes. Once he stopped and shifted gears, and it seemed to Tom that he could hear the pleasant gurgle of slow-running water. It was growing warmer now and he could feel the sunlight glowing on his bare arms and one of his hands.

There was song in the air, he thought. The crickets were beginning their chorus for the day. A bobwhite whistled from a field as they passed, and Tom resisted an impulse to whistle back. For with the climbing of the unseen sun, he found his courage climbing, too. And with it, he thought, that strange sense of achievement that comes when all that has been disparate and chaotic falls inexorably into place. The fragments of the story were connecting in his mind just as the structure of a puzzle or a game of chess or a cryptogram comes clear at last to the one who has stayed with it for long enough.

First, he thought, we have the professor from Weimar, the specialist in Christian iconology who also turned out to have been a specialist of sorts in the corruption of young men. Or was it the other way—with the young men corrupting him? Whichever it was, it led to his dismissal from the university, as Junius had said, and it was easy enough to imagine the clucking tongues of his former colleagues, and his gradual or swift descent to the back streets of Berlin.

Second, Otto, the blackbrowed Croatian. A Communist, Summers had called him. It could be that his politics gave him the idea of victimizing the Church, of making off with some of the immense wealth that this great institution had amassed through the better part of two thousand years. How the scheme developed was anybody's guess. But the key to its success was obviously someone who could do the research necessary to determine the exact locations of the treasures of religious art. Then the problem became one of color photography and the clever duplication of the originals in glass and base metals. After that it was not easy—none of it was easy—but clearly it had been possible to substitute the replicas for the originals, break up the crowns and mitres, and send the precious stones overseas to be recut by Junius and disposed of through trustworthy fences to buyers over here. Lapidaries like old Junius would have been easy enough to come by—say two or three for the price of a Dutch guilder—in the diamond marts of the Netherlands.

So the scheme was launched, although they must have needed a stake to start from, and a super-burglar or two to handle the European, African, and Middle Eastern end of the operation. A few efficiently planned and flawlessly executed bank robberies could have set them up in ready cash.

And you had a first-rate training ground for thieves on a continent that was crawling with unemployed spies like Ehrendt or Kröger or some of the other criminal Übermenschen that old Colonel Webb of G-2, Seventh Army, used to love to reminisce about.

From that point the rest was easy enough to imagine, thought Tom. One day some years back the courtly Doctor Summers appeared (no doubt with a forged passport) in a real estate office in Martha's Vineyard. He soon contracted for the purchase of the somewhat run-down property on Water Street in Edgartown. Money was no problem, to the delight of the Yankee builders who did the work. He was willing to spend lavishly to convert the old-fashioned house into a kind of fortress, even though outwardly it had seemed only a place suitable for a man of scholarly inclinations, living quietly in semi-retirement, with a basement suite ostensibly for a serving-maid but in fact for the unseen old artisan whose labors would help to keep the money flowing in. And with a dour chauffeur-gardener to attend to the doctor's daily needs.

Yet not all his needs. For in the course of his investigations at Harvard, the professor acquired a student assistant named Starr, a handsome kid by all accounts, including Helen Mahoney's, gifted but self-indulgent, and easy enough to corrupt. Or, thought Tom, to be corrupted by. But the problem was that Freddy was unwilling to stay where he belonged. As soon as he was graduated, he followed his friend to the Vineyard, and from Otto's point of view turned from being a professor's helper into a downright threat.

Look, thought Tom. Here's Otto, with a smoothly working scheme. Any interloper who found out too much about it could leak the details. And here came this long-lashed, long-haired boy into the island picture. What would you do if you were Otto? Obviously, eliminate him. The murder of this fair youth could serve a double or a triple purpose: one, to get rid of a threat without harm to the academic goose that laid the golden eggs; two, to discourage Summers from further dangerous dalliances; and three—this above all—to protect the scheme from discovery.

All right. You have the motive for the murder of Freddy Starr. But what about its savagery? How about the painting of the face? Here you had to speculate, but the grounds, once you had named them, seemed clear enough: a combination of fear and jealousy seething in the brain of a psychopathic personality. Otto, say, discovers the pair making their kind of love, and strangles one lover to save the other on whom the continuance of the scheme depends. Searching Freddy's clothes and pockets for marks that would betray his identity, he finds a lipstick, and, in the crudest of crude humors, knowing the name chosen by the emergent nation of homosexuals, he paints the gay head design on Freddy's face in angry, slashing strokes. There, Summers, look. There's your gay boy. How do you like him now?

Then what about the beheading? Why that? Again, thought Tom, it's a mixture of motives. First anger, probably—the same sort of anger that causes rapists to slash and mutilate their victims. Second, the necessity for concealment. The plan forms in his mind. Bury the head in the woods nearby. Weight the body and sink it far off in the deep waters of the sound. Separate the two and you lessen the possibility of certain identification.

So that was it. Or that could be it. Just at dusk on the afternoon after the midnight murder, Otto wraps the head and body in the tarp, lifts it into the back of the pickup, and takes off for the shore. On the way through the woods he stops to bury the head. Then, as night falls, he stops again on the road above the cliffs. It is the loneliest place he knows on the island. Dropping the body over the edge will save him the trouble of a far longer carry. Later that night he will come in the speedboat, retrieve it, weight it, sink it in the sea. Even if the weights come loose and the body is eventually washed up somewhere, the absence of the head will make identification next to impossible.

A good scheme. Not as good as the scheme of the jewels, but good enough. Except that, like all schemes, it had its flaws. Otto in his rage reckoned without a man and a dog. How could he know that Nix, coursing through the woods, would nose out and dig up the buried head? And how could he know that there was someone on the lonely beach near Gay Head the night he dumped the body over the cliff to the beach? He didn't, thought Tom triumphantly. He didn't know until he saw my flashlight and—dimly—the figure of a man in the act of discovering a headless corpse. That was his mistake: not checking the beach. And my mistake was in ever supposing that the hurler of the corpse was trying to scare me off. He was still too blind in his murderous rage even to suspect that I was there. And that careless act set in motion a train of circumstances that would oblige him to murder twice more in order to protect his scheme from discovery.

The rocking and bumping motions stopped at last and the engine wheezed once and died. In the hard steel bed of the truck, Tom lay waiting for what he knew might come next —another murder and another body-dumping—though this time in cold blood and with better advance planning. But his exuberance, strangely, was still alive. Whatever they do now, he thought, they are beaten, their scheme becomes inoperative, starting today. For Polly will have found Milliken, Milliken will have found Junius, and Junius will have set them on the trail to this place. Or would he? The house-ridden old man in carpet slippers, the man who could not tell high tide from low, might very well know absolutely nothing about this end of the operation.

Powerful hands that could only have been Otto's lifted him clear of the truck and lowered him to the grass. But the hands that unbound his scarf from his eyes were those of Summers, who stood now above him looking down.

"You are covered with dust," he said. "Even your hair is prematurely gray. But at least, now, you will be able to see again."

Tom nodded without speaking. Five feet away in the blinding sunlight stood Otto, watching them. On a leather sling over his shoulder he held a tommy gun, his fingers hooked in the strap.

"Where is your knife?" asked Summers. "Give me your knife to cut the ropes."

"We do not cut the ropes," said Otto. "Keep him tied and there is no worry. We will only have to tie him up again tonight."

"What does he mean?" asked Tom quietly.

"For the boat tonight," Summers said.

"What boat?"

"The boat we will summon when it is time. To take you away from this island."

"Why? They will stop you. The island is patrolled."

"If they try to stop us, they will die, as before. You, too."

"Does Otto mean to kill me?"

"Possibly," said Summers. "I hope not. He has killed too much. But with Otto one is never entirely certain."

Chapter Eight

1

THE TRUCK had stopped in the midst of a small clearing that strangely reminded him of the hiding place he had imagined long ago. Crowding in from all sides were tall pines and oaks and at the far end of the open space stood a hip-roofed cabin of weathered gray shingle. Otto now sat smoking on a bench under an oak tree, his back against the bole, his booted feet stretched out, the gun beside him. Spread as if to dry outside the door of the cabin was the tarpaulin, the only visible sign that this had been the place of Freddy's murder and Otto's savage butchery.

Tom rolled his body until he could look in the direction of the road the truck had followed. It was only a lane, a path among the crowding trees. From the angle of the sun it was clear that it must run vaguely southward, though he remembered the dozens of twists and turns of the journey between the barn and this forsaken cabin. The sound of running water he had heard could only have been a stream from an inland source crossing the roadbed. Somewhere to the south lay the sea, but here there was no fragrance of salt air: only the odors of dry grass and pine needles.

They had reported finding fragments of pitch at the base of Freddy's neck and Tom himself had seen pine needles in the hair of the severed head. The disputed tarp was here and a little searching would doubtless uncover Otto's ax. And from here, near dusk of a day less than two weeks ago, would have begun the trip to the cliffs with Freddy's corpse. How long a trip? There was no way of knowing. But he remembered the pine groves along the South Road a few rods east of Cora's house where Nix had appeared with his trophy. It could be that this clearing lay somewhere back of that.

He rolled back until he could face Otto, who watched him with eyes narrowed to slits under the visor of the long-billed cap.

"Loosen the ropes on my ankles," he said.

"What for?"

"They're cutting off circulation."

"Too bad," Otto said. "Do you have to circulate?"

"I want to go for water," said Tom. "My throat is dry."

"From fear," said Otto, grinning. "Fear dries the throat. But you will find no water here."

"We crossed a stream on the way to this place."

"It is far away," Otto said. "And I would not let you go there, anyway. You might try to run and then I would have to kill you. Besides, the stream is no good for drinking—unless you are an animal. Polluted, you understand? Poisoned. Ask the professor."

Summers had emerged from the woods behind the cabin. "If you wish to relieve yourself—" he said to Tom.

Tom shook his head. "Not now. I was asking for water."

"There is coffee in the truck," said Summers.

"All right."

Otto was still grinning. "You asked for water," he said. "I did not hear you mention coffee."

"Coffee will do," said Tom. "Unless it is poisoned."

"Give him some coffee," said Otto gleefully. "Let us see

if it poisons him. It would save us much trouble." The joke pleased him and he laughed aloud.

Croatian wit, thought Tom. Hillbilly humor from the Yugoslav mountains. Summers unscrewed the cup from the thermos, filled it half full, and held it to Tom's lips. The coffee was lukewarm and rank, but he drank it all.

"This is all we can offer you," said Summers mildly.

"Just a little poison," grinned Otto. "How do you feel now?"

"Like relieving myself," said Tom.

"The professor will carry you," said Otto. "Or else he will help with your clothes and you can do it here. He is the captain in charge of relief. He relieves you with coffee. He helps you to relieve yourself." Otto was grinning broadly.

"Never mind," said Tom. "Perhaps later."

"You hear that, Professor?" railed Otto. "He does not trust you. He is afraid of what might happen if he relieves himself in your presence. Not now, he says. He is wise. He is wiser than dear Friedrich. Young man, did you ever hear of poor Friedrich?"

Tom glared in his direction. "Plenty," he said shortly. "From you. In the barn. More than enough."

"You see, Professor?" said Otto. "He has heard of Friedrich. He knows what happened to Friedrich. He does not wish to share the fate of Friedrich."

"Shut your filthy mouth," said Summers disgustedly. To Tom he said: "There is a bunk in the cabin. I will have him carry you there if you wish. Then you will be away from his dirty jokes."

Under the bill of the cap Otto's eyes had narrowed again. "If I take you in there," he told Tom coldly, "do not try to escape. You will only die as your friends died at sea." He picked up the gun and cradled it in his arms. "I have here a friend with a loud voice. His teeth are sharper than arrows. One word from me and he will tear you to pieces."

When Tom nodded, he set the gun on the bench and rose, stretching his arms. "All right. We go." He lifted Tom over one shoulder, strode to the cabin, and dumped him onto the stained mattress in the wooden bunk. "Go to sleep, baby," he said. "Later we will take you for a ride." He went out again to resume his seat on the bench under the oak.

The cabin, Tom saw, was sparsely furnished. Against one wall stood a decrepit kitchen chair. On a table just inside the door was the only modern piece of equipment: a portable shortwave transmitter with receiving attachment, battery operated. So this was the voice of their command post in the island wilderness. This was the way they had been reaching the boat offshore. Smash it, somehow, and they could not summon the boat tonight. Yes, he thought. Smash it and Otto will be there in the doorway spraying the interior of the cabin with lead.

He lay back on the musty-smelling mattress and idly watched a spider completing his web in a corner of the window above his head. Sleep, Otto had said, but he did not feel drowsy. Perhaps Otto would sleep on his bench by the tree. Like me, Tom thought, he was up all night, and it must be nearly noon. If he really slept, and if I could get clear of these ropes, there might be a chance of getting away through the woods behind this shack. If Otto slept. If it weren't for the ropes. If. If. The word was like a spike, puncturing his courage. He could almost hear it whistling away, like air from a tire. If.

By twisting his body and raising his head he could see Otto's booted feet. If Summers was in the clearing at all, he was out of Tom's line of vision. Perhaps, knowing that they must wait through the long afternoon until they could move out with their prisoner under cover of darkness, and knowing also that Otto was on guard with the gun, Summers had chosen this moment for a noonday siesta.

A queer one, thought Tom. Since that first interview in the basement store-room, he had evidently done his best to be kind. It was he who had refused to let Tom's eyes be taped, he who had suggested the back seat rather than the trunk of the Mercedes, he who had remembered the coffee in the thermos. Had he done these acts from charity, like old Junius with the water and the pillow, or was it only his way of showing how much more decent, how much less barbarous he was than Otto—a means of differentiating himself from the callous murderer, reasserting in this way at least something of his former dignity as a scholar and, in a manner of speaking, a gentleman? Whatever his motives, he was nowhere to be seen.

Some crawling creature, probably a beetle, was making its way up the side of Tom's neck. He shook his head vigorously but it would not be dislodged. He raised his legs together and using his buttocks as a fulcrum rocked up to a sitting position, his back against the fly-strewn sill of the window. By leaning far to the right he could see that Otto was still sitting on the bench, the gun within his easy reach, its metal glinting dully in the sun. He had pulled the visor of his cap low over his eyes to cut out the glare. Asleep? It was impossible to tell. Or how quick on the trigger if he came suddenly awake. Tom shook his head again. The beetle was now crawling inside the collar of his shirt.

It was then that he felt the window behind him being slowly raised, and heard the breathing whisper that could only be that of Summers.

"No sound," it said. "Move just enough to let me reach

the rope on your wrists. I have no knife, only Otto's ax. Let me see what I can do. If he wakes, we are dead."

Tom nodded, stretching his wrists as far back as they would go.

"All right," said Summers. "Be still now and let me work."

2

She had been parked on the shoulder of the road for more than an hour before she saw the squad car coming back. Milliken, recognizing her, pulled up with a crunch of tires on the roadside gravel.

"You're not supposed—" he began, leaning out.

"I know," said Polly. "I'm not supposed to be here. I'm supposed to be back in the house twiddling my thumbs while you—"

"While I miss the boat or the bus or whatever you call it," said Milliken morosely.

"The Mercedes?"

"Lost it somewhere up island. Went all the way to Gay Head. No Mercedes."

"So it must have turned off the road."

"Unless they took to the water," said Milliken. "But I don't think they'd try that."

"Where are you going now?"

"To meet the others at the airport. What they call a posse in the westerns. They should be there by now. We're going to check every goddam side road between here and Chilmark."

"That's a lot of goddam side roads," said Polly.

"That's why we have a lot of people," Milliken said. "Except Harry Royce. It's his day off. It would be, the day of a manhunt, and I can't find him anywhere. His wife thinks he went fishing, but she's not sure. Might even be over in Wood's Hole. So that's no help."

"Maybe I could find him," said Polly.

"Nope," said Milliken. "I don't want you around the roads in a shoot-out, if we have one. No, I'll tell you one thing that will help and that's that it rained less than twenty-four hours ago. We're counting on tire-marks. The Mercedes has a herring-bone tread."

"Let me come with you," said Polly.

"You can follow me to the airport," Milliken said. "They say they're sending a helicopter from Hyannis to search from the air."

"I could go with him," said Polly. "Up there would be safe."

"Come along and we'll see," Milliken said.

Milliken had just turned into the second lane past West Tisbury when the shortwave crackled and a voice said, "Calling Car One." He jammed on the brakes, picked up the microphone, and acknowledged.

"Gilbert here," said the voice. "I've got treadmarks."

"V-shaped? Like chevrons?"

"Something like chevrons," Gilbert said.

"All right. Where are you?"

"I make it almost exactly two and two tenths miles beyond Tisbury heading west. Lieutenant, do you know that road that connects the South Road to the Middle Road?

Just a couple hundred yards beyond that. Old apple orchard. Do I go in or wait?"

"Wait," said Milliken. "I'll be there. While you're waiting, tell the others."

"Will do," Gilbert said happily.

Milliken drove as fast as he dared without using the siren until he reached Gilbert's car on the road shoulder, its blue light revolving. "Why the light?" he asked, getting out.

"For the chopper," said Gilbert, a tall, eager young man with a deep sunburn. "To show him we've found the place where the car turned off."

Milliken squinted at the sky. "Where is he now?"

"He already went past," Gilbert said glumly.

"Never mind," Milliken said. "He'll be back and scare the hell out of me and you and the people we're after. Who thought up that one about the helicopter?"

"It was my idea," said Gilbert, flushing under his tan.

"Never mind," said Milliken again. "Where'd you see the treadmarks?"

"Right up that dirt road," Gilbert said, pointing. "It's black-topped for twenty yards and after that it's dirt. Here, I'll show you."

"Never mind," said Milliken. "I believe you."

"So what do we do?" asked Gilbert.

"You get in here and unpack your thirty-eight and leave the safety on and we'll go exploring," Milliken said.

"What about the light?"

"Leave her going," Milliken said. "Maybe the chopper will come back."

From behind, thought Polly, the pilot's hair looked exactly like a black bristle brush. They were skimming low, a hundred yards above the treetops, and following the winding ribbon of the South Road where it angled between Menemsha and Squibnocket Ponds. The ponds were much larger than they looked from the ground, but no bigger than puddles beside the vast Atlantic, which from this height resembled elephant-hide. If elephants were blue, she thought.

And why are you up here thinking about hairbrushes and puddles and elephant-hide, she asked herself, when Tom is somewhere down there, maybe hurt, maybe even dead, and they can't find the damned Mercedes and here it is almost noon and I watched them leave in the car before dawn, and they had Tom with them. The old man in the house said they had Tom with them, and who knows where they've got him now? Tears welled in her eyes, but she squeezed them dry and leaned forward to punch the pilot's sloping shoulder. "Let's go back," she yelled through the beat of the rotor, and pointed eastward along the curving coast.

The boy with the brush cut nodded energetically to show that he had heard and cupped a hand around his mouth for a shouted reply. But his words were drowned in the pulsing roar and it was only when he dipped and turned that she knew he had heard and agreed.

Where the farmhouse had stood there was now only a fieldstone chimney like an arthritic finger pointing at the sky. At the edge of the meadow across the road the barn had survived, decrepit but intact. Through its open door they could see the Mercedes, buff-colored in the gloom. Milliken stopped the squad car and got out, the service pistol in his hand.

"Get out on your side," he told Gilbert. "Take the mike and tell them we've found the Mercedes and where. Tell them not to come in here until I give them the word. Then you stay here and cover me. I'm going to have a look."

He angled toward the barn, flattened his back against the weathered siding, and stepped suddenly through the yawning door. Except for the shrilling of the crickets, there was only silence. The car, he found, was unlocked, but the keys were gone. He climbed the worn rungs for a look at the disused haymow, sneezed in the rising dust, and jumped down. Nothing held his attention for long until he had nearly completed his circuit of the floor. Then he knelt suddenly beside the oil-smear far back in the barn, touched it with a finger, sniffed at the smudge, and wiped his fingertip on one of the unstained planks. He strode back to the Mercedes, released the handbrake, heaved and pushed until the car rolled backwards, and saw the second oil-stain. Either they sometimes park the Mercedes back there, he thought, or else we have a two-car proposition.

He walked slowly back to the squad car, his eyes vainly scanning the ground for any tell-tale sign.

"What did you find?" asked Gilbert.

"The Mercedes unlocked but the car key gone. Also two oil stains on the flooring in different parts of the barn. It looks like two cars. It looks as if they left one here and took off in the other."

For a long minute he stood gazing at the sunlit branches of the trees. "Gilbert," he said at last, "let's try it this way. You pick up the mike and tell the boys to come up here now. But walking, not riding. There'll be two sets of treadmarks along the road—the Mercedes and ours. Tell them to see if they can find another set."

"And what if they don't?" asked Gilbert intently.

"We'll spread out here and comb the ground until we locate something. Tell them that. No. Here. Let's have that mike. I'll tell them."

Sitting behind the wheel of his old model Plymouth parked along the shoulder of the Middle Road, Harry Royce reached over to the glove compartment for a cigarette. It was here that the helicopter had spotted him, turned back in its course, and dipped low over the car, with the deafening roar and the airstream from the rotors like a hurricane. He had to stop and get out and wave to them before they rose again and went zooming off to the east. For a brief moment he had looked up into the pilot's face, astonishingly near, topped with wind-whipped black hair and masked with sunglasses. Looking up had made him dizzy and he did not want to drive again until it passed. He found the box and shook out a cigarette and lighted it.

"Fan out," Milliken told them. "They're gone, but not the way they came in. Go in pairs and start from the barn. You're looking for any path a car could follow. It could be a jeep. Look for treadmarks on gravel or sand."

"I'll go with you," Gilbert said.

They were eight in all. Almost at once a trooper named Todd from Falmouth waved vigorously from the site of the farmhouse and Milliken ran to his side.

Todd had plucked a handful of timothy. The brown tops of the grass were lightly smeared with black oil.

"Good," said Milliken. "Move out from here. Over there looks like some kind of a passage."

Just as he spoke they heard the helicopter returning. "Damn," he said. "One of you guys get over there in the barnyard and wave him off."

It came in so close over their heads that they could read the numbers. The man on the ground pumped his arms frantically and pointed east. The pilot swerved and obediently departed, the steady beat of his rotors slowly dissipating in the bright air.

Just then they heard the tommy gun in the distance. One burst, an interval, and another longer burst. Then silence.

"Over there," said Milliken, pointing. "Keep ten yards apart and move in slow. Stop behind trees when you can and cover for the next man. All right, now, move out."

3

Royce finished the cigarette, ground it out in the ashtray, broke open the butt, powdered the tobacco in his palm, rolled the patch of paper into a tiny ball, and dropped the debris from the car window. Just like the sergeant told us, he thought with a grin, from the time we was drafted to the time we hit Sicily. He laughed once at the recollection—a single bark that sounded like *huh*—and had just reached for the ignition key when the truck went roaring past.

It was doing about eighty and headed west. "In a hurry," Royce said aloud. "Speed demon." Etched in his memory was the fleeting picture of the black-browed driver hunched over the wheel. Flag him down when he comes back, he thought, and give him a ticket. He started the car, made a leisurely U-turn, and set off in slow pursuit. The truck, a gray-painted pickup, was still in distant view when he topped the rise of ground by Menemsha Pond, and he saw it turn left into Moshup's Trail. Four minutes later Royce took the same curve at fifty-five and gained speed going down the hill. If he stays on this road, I'll get him, he thought. Or else at Gay Head.

Milliken stopped his men at the edge of the clearing and stood gazing across at the gray-shingled cabin at the far end. The door was open and the whole place was quiet as a graveyard.

"Looks like they've gone," he told Gilbert, "but I'll have to check it out. Now get this. Nobody shoots nobody. Just be ready. Pass the word along."

Gilbert nodded and moved off to the right. Milliken kept left along the line of trees to the rear of the cabin. Gilbert watched him duck below the window, round the corner, and enter the doorway, gun first. He reappeared at once and waved them in, stooping to pick up something from the ground.

"What's that you got?" asked Gilbert.

Milliken held out his hand, palm up. "Empties from the tommy gun," he said. "Bet you a dollar it's the same gun that killed Hupp and Whitehead. But all they did here was shoot up their own wireless."

"Where's the car, then?" cried Gilbert. "They couldn't get out of here. We had them blocked."

"Another road," said Milliken. "Every woodchuck knows that. Come on, let's find that other road."

It was Gilbert who found it first, but it was not a road. He stood with open mouth gazing down at the bullet-torn jacket, the paisley scarf, and the bloody astonished upturned face.

Milliken saw him and went over.

"Who is it?" said Gilbert. "Anybody you know?"

Milliken nodded. "Man named Summers from Edgar-

175

town," he said. "The car's gone, and the big guy that drives it. Now where the hell is Tom Cook?"

Royce was still more than a mile behind the truck when he saw it turn toward the shore on the new gravel road that led down to the dunes. He knew the place well enough. Back in April a bulldozer had worked in there for most of a week, gouging the road and leveling a gravel flat at the bottom as a parking place for summer people who wanted to swim.

Got him bottled up now, he thought gleefully. Watch him wilt when I pull in there and hand him a ticket for speeding.

He stopped the car at the top of the rise and looked down. The truck was parked on the yellow gravel far below. From this height it looked empty. He's gone down to fish or take a leak or walk on the beach, thought Royce.

The high dune blocked his view of the shoreline, but he did not worry. He lighted a cigarette, reached for the summons-pad in the glove compartment, filled in the date and the nature of the infraction, and at last strolled down to get the license number of the pickup, copying it carefully in the space provided. The key was gone from the ignition and the truck was completely empty. It was also practically new: either a late '67 or one of the first they had put out in '68. No rust to speak of and the rubber in good shape. Sometimes they kept the registration in the glove compartment, but it, too, was empty.

A sandy path led up over the dune from the parking place and Royce slowly climbed it, pausing to pluck and crush a bayberry leaf between his fingers, sniffing it appreciatively as he climbed. It was warm in the sun. He could feel the sand sifting over his shoe-tops, and at the crest of the dune he was breathing hard.

What he saw from there stopped him in his tracks. As automatically as any other infantry veteran cresting a rise, he dropped to the sand and slid backward until his head was on a level with the waving sea-grass. A hundred yards offshore lay a forty-foot motorboat, her engines idling. From the dinghy alongside a tall man in a long-visored cap was climbing aboard. While Royce watched, two crewmen hoisted and shipped the dinghy, turning it upside down on the broad after-deck, even as the cruiser gunned her motors and turned her nose toward the broad reach between No Man's Land and Cuttyhunk. She was half a mile offshore when Royce stood up, brushed the sand from his pants and sweater, and walked back to the parking-lot.

Gone fishing, he thought. Late for a fishing-date and drives eighty miles an hour to get there. One thing he's going to catch when he gets back is a nice little summons. Using the fender of the pickup as a desk he signed his name with a flourish, checked the carbon copy, tore off the top sheet, and slid it under the windshield wiper. Something was nibbling at the edges of his mind but he could not place his finger on it. When he got back to his own car at the top of the rise the cruiser was nearly out of sight in the glistening water to the west.

Tom, at that moment, was emerging from the woods a mile east of the cabin, with a scratch on his forehead from a pine bough and a gash in one leg from the strand of rusty barbed wire that had sent him sprawling on the far side of the brook. The ugly echoes of the gunbursts were still fresh in his memory and he crossed the pasture at a lope and did not slow down until he had vaulted the low stone wall onto the blacktopped highway that could only be the South Road.

Now for the first time he could smell the breeze from the sea—like a benison, he thought, after the tangle of the pinewoods and the sucking bog he had waded through in the flight from Otto.

He found that he knew the part of the road where he stood and turned east for Tisbury and the telephone at the general store. First Milliken, he thought, and then Polly—unless I can get them both at once. She would certainly have called Milliken, might in fact have driven to the sub-station at Oak Bluffs, might even now be sitting in that office with the rank smell of coffee and the perpetual droning chatter of the shortwave set in the corner.

But Milliken would not be there. Somewhere on the island, cruising fast, either alone or with Royce, he would be trailing the fugitives, and with very little information to go on. Old Junius, assuming they had found him, could hardly have helped. He had been in the basement workshop when the Mercedes left the house in the dark of early morning, and the only clue to the direction Otto had taken was inside Tom's head.

One good sign was the helicopter. Twice during his flight through the woods, he had heard its plosive beat, racketing westward and then coming back. For what it was worth, they were searching from the air—unless the ship had only been making a routine patrol of the island coastline. All I can do is guess, he thought, and I choose to guess they were out looking for me, and of course the conspirators, that curious international pair, wedded by years of mutual hatred and common cause, though no one knows but me the exact nature of their marriage. No one else, either, knows who murdered Freddy Starr, and why. No one else knows who killed Monty Hupp and young Whitehead.

Get there, he urged himself. Get there to the telephone

and tell them the story while there's still time. He began to
run again along the shoulder of the road.

A car was coming fast on his side of the highway and he
stepped back to let it pass. But it slowed and stopped with a
screech of brakes, and he saw that Polly was at the wheel.

She came to him quietly and put her arms around his
neck. "Your forehead's cut. You're hurt, Tom," she said.

"I grazed a tree in the woods," he said. "How are you?"

"I've never been happier. Or luckier."

"Or noisier," said Tom, grinning. "You ought to fix
those squeaky brakes."

"I will," she said, kissing him repeatedly. "But not now.
I'm otherwise occupied. Oh, Tom, I'm so glad you're all
right."

"Where's Milliken?" he asked.

"Down the road with his men. They found Dr. Summers."

"Where was he?"

"In the woods. Killed. They think Otto did it. They're
bringing out the body."

"What about Otto?"

"Gone," she said. "They don't know where he is. Oh,
Tom, come on. Get in. We've got to go and tell Milliken
you're safe."

4

Royce leaned forward and shut off the tape recorder. "I
guess that winds it up," he said. "For you, I mean. You're a

free man. Milliken's putting your name in for a medal."

"For what?"

"For catching them."

"I was the one that got caught," said Tom, grinning. "You and Milliken get the medals."

"I got me a medal," Royce said. "Now I just got to sit down here and put my story on the tape. My problem is how to say it without sounding like a moron."

"You'd never laid eyes on Otto," said Tom. "How could you know the man you were chasing was a murderer?"

"I shoulda guessed," Royce said. "Man drives eighty mile an hour, parks the truck, gets aboard a cruiser. I figured he was going fishing. And o' course that's what they said they was doing when the Coast Guard caught up with them over there in the Elizabeth Islands. That's where they made their big mistake, farting around inside there when they shoulda gone right out to sea."

"Otto would have been caught sooner or later. With those forged passports, I don't see how they got away with it as long as they did."

"Easier than you'd think," Royce said. "They was so sure of themselves he and the professor had already started taking out citizenship papers. Tom, I'm telling you, you can get away with anything."

"Maybe for a while."

"For a good while. Like that Freddy."

"What about Freddy?"

"We just got it from Boston. Seems a couple of years back he was picked up in a ladies' room wearing women's clothes. What's that they call it?"

"Transvestite?"

"That's it. Freddy got away with that. Case was hushed up."

"Freddy was born to lose."

"I believe that," Royce said seriously. "I seen them in the war. Born winners. Born losers. Sometimes the losers win a while. But they're born to lose. So they end up losing."

Tom got up and stretched his arms, yawning widely. "If we're finished here," he said, "I'll go along back to Edgartown."

"Like I told you, you're free as a bird," Royce said. "Got your bike?"

"Thanks to you," said Tom. "Did they ever catch the thin man?"

"Not yet," said Royce. "Could be they never will."

"Are you coming over?"

"Not now. Milliken's still there. I'm covering here."

Milliken heard the motorcycle in the driveway and came out to stand on the granite steps. "All done now?" he asked.

"It's all on the tape," said Tom. "Where's Polly?"

"Gone to the store," Milliken said. "Back in ten minutes. She thought I looked hungry."

"You do."

"Well, I'm not. I'll eat at the Sea Gull when I get through here. The old man was asking for you. He wants to see you."

"Where is he?"

"Inside. In the library. I'll see you sometime tomorrow. OK?"

"I'll be there," said Tom. "I want to return that pistol."

Junius rose and came forward as Tom entered—very small, very pale, with the tonsured ring of frosty hair. "Please sit down," he said. "I am glad you escaped from Otto."

"I was lucky."

"It also took skill," Junius said. "But they have him safe now, isn't that so?"

"In jail in Boston."

"What will they do with him?"

"Try him for murder. Probably."

"Why not certainly?"

"There are technical problems. They may deport him."

"They will also deport me?"

"Perhaps. But with you, there are extenuating circumstances. You were a prisoner in this house. You did your work, but you could not get away."

"That is the other thing I wished to speak about."

"What is that?"

"My work. The stones, precious stones. You are sympathetic."

"Not very."

"How could that be?"

"They're beautiful, some of them. But they're also hard and cold, like what happened here."

"You are right about the beauty," said Junius softly. "Even the names are poetry. Turquoise, ruby, chalcedony. Lapis lazuli, aquamarine. And, like poetry, immortal."

"That is a poetical way of speaking," said Tom. "Not really immortal."

"Such beauty, preserved, is a form of immortality in the material world."

"I can remember arguing some such point," said Tom. "The question was how something that is not alive, and never has been alive, can be called immortal. Keats's urn, for example."

"I do not know this Keats. But I know that precious stones are immortal."

"Buried in the ground and forgotten," said Tom gently. "Lost in shipwreck. Destroyed by fire."

"Yes, yes," said Junius impatiently. "Yet they come again to light the world. Out of the ground and the old graves. Up from the bottom of the sea and even from the ashes of the fire. Many are hidden, many stolen, many removed from their former settings."

"The crowns and the ikons," said Tom.

"Yes," said Junius, unaware of any irony. "The old crowns, the hilts of swords, the ancient shields and bucklers. But think, Mr. Cook, they are always somewhere. Who can say but that still on this globe are not the gems that Cleopatra wore, or the Queen of Sheba, or Solomon in his glory? That is immortality. I have held it in these hands."

"You speak of immortality," said Tom. "I want to speak of its opposite. Here, on this island, four men died. Two of them were good men."

Junius sat silent, gazing at the floor, his hands quiescent in his lap. "I know about mortality," he presently said. "At my age it is felt daily in the bones. And of course you are right. But about the stones I am right, also."

"I'll give you that," said Tom, getting up, "if you'll grant me the other. And thank you for helping me."

"How? How did I help you? I wish to know."

"With the water and the pillow," said Tom.

"Oh, that," said Junius disappointedly. "It was nothing. You are welcome. I would do it again."

"I hope you never have to," said Tom, lightly. He left the old man sitting in the quiet room, crossed to the door, and went out.

The sun, far in the west, was gilding the windows of Polly's house. He saw that she was there, waiting beside the car, her dark hair winnowed by the breeze off the channel. He went across the smooth lawn to her side.

"So you're free," she said.

"Until Otto's trial, anyhow. It feels good." He took her hand. "Where shall we go with our freedom?"

"Wherever you like."

"How about Gay Head, where it all began?"

"It began for me here," said Polly. "On the porch of this house."

"For me, too," he said. "I was thinking of the other. Let's do both."

"Both what?"

"Go out there and then come back here."

"All right," she said. "We can park at the top by the old lighthouse and hold hands and look across at Cuttyhunk."

"Cuttyhunk," said Tom. "Did I ever ask you about Cuttyhunk?"

"Yes, you did," said Polly. "Out there at the picnic. Then I didn't know about it, but now I do."

"How do you know?"

"I found a man who knew. Very nice man. A minister from Pocasset. A friend of Letitia's. The Reverend Mr. Percy Rex."

"And what was his idea?"

"He said no one really knows. It's from an Indian word that none of the settlers could even begin to spell. But one of its meanings, they think, is 'point of departure.' "

"That's good," said Tom. "It fits us right now."

"Doesn't it?" said Polly. "He told me another that was better." She started the car.

"Tell me."

"He said it meant an experience entirely surrounded by water. Isn't that perfect?"

"You're perfect," Tom said, laughing. "Let's take your perfection and go out there and look across at Cuttyhunk."

"And hold hands," said Polly. "Remember that. And then come back here."

"Yes," he said, "and then come back here."

VJG   GPF

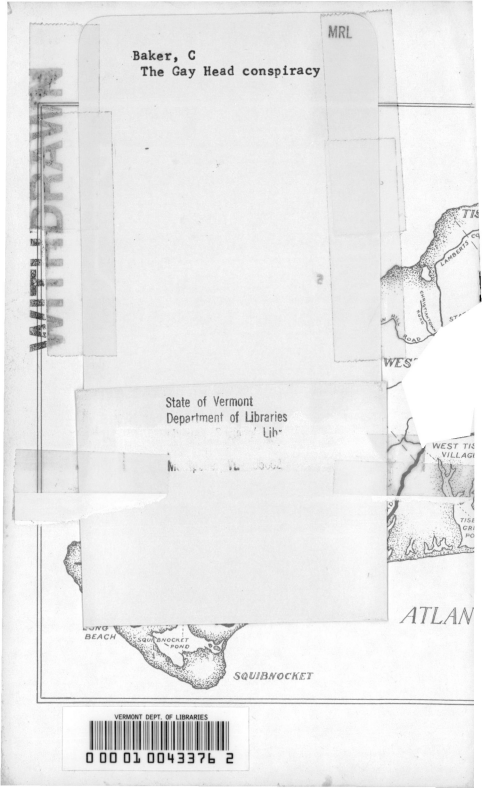